The Irish Maiden

R.J. Groves

Copyright © 2018 by R.J. Groves
Edited by Graham Toseland
ISBN: 978 0 6452675 2 5
Groves Publishing
Formats available: ebook, Paperback

About the author

Australian author R.J. Groves has been passionate about writing since she could put pen to paper and can usually be found jotting plots and stories down on anything she can get her hands on. Describing herself as a mum, wife, author, and coffee lover, her other passions include music, cooking, books, adventures, and searching for plot bunnies in even the most mundane activities.

Facebook: facebook.com/rjgauthor
Instagram: instagram.com/r.j.groves_author
Twitter: twitter.com/rjg_author
Website: www.rjgrovesauthor.com

Books by R. J. Groves

The Bridal Shop series
Save the Date
Be My Valentine
Say You'll Be Mine

Jilted Brides series
Finding a Bride
Written in the Sand

Cities of the World series
In Paris
The Irish Maiden

Set Ups series
The Set Up

Mail Order Brides series
The Calm in the Storm
The Warmth in the Winter
The Song in the Silence

Standalones
Writing You
Two Babies Too Many
Second Chance
The Boyfriend Application
Sweeter Things
Home Bound
Stay With Me
Her First Noel
When Dreams Come True
To Fall For You

To Abigail, for being my sunshine.

The Irish Maiden

R.J. Groves

Prologue

'So, there really is only one thing left to say,' Alex said, concluding his best-man speech. He looked towards Scott and Olivia. 'Scott, farewell buddy. It was nice knowing you.' He paused, the crowd erupting in laughter, before leaning back towards the microphone. 'But seriously, I wish you all the best in your new life with your beautiful bride.' He held up his glass. 'To the bride and groom!'

Everyone chorused his toast as he moved towards the bar, the DJ calling up the bride and groom for their first dance. He ordered a shot of whiskey, neat, and felt his pocket for the papers he'd been carrying around. He may be at his best friend's wedding and may have just given the best and funniest best-man speech anyone here would have ever heard in their lives, but partying was far from what he really wanted to do. Especially with Betty, his recent ex, sitting on the opposite side of the room with the guy she left him for.

The bartender placed the whiskey in front of him and he downed it in one go, pulling a face at the burn it left as it travelled down his throat. He knew there was a reason he never drank whiskey.

'That was some speech.'

And then, there was Liz. He ordered another and turned to face Elizabeth Henders—Scott's sister and the girl he secretly dated for a few months before moving to Paris. She was as beautiful as ever. And completely off limits since, when he tried to come clean about their relationship, Scott said he would kill him if he ever got involved with his sister. It was just as well, anyway. Liz deserved way better than him.

'Hello, Liz,' he said. 'It's been a while.'

'It didn't have to be.'

'You know why I couldn't call, Liz.'

Because he would have changed his mind.

She nodded. It had been a mutual decision. Scott and his parents had been like family to Alex. He couldn't lose his best friend and certainly couldn't allow himself to come between Liz and Scott. It was for the best. And he was sure he took it harder than she did.

'Are you ready to join the bride and groom on the dancefloor?' she asked, her tone light.

He smiled at her, picking up the refilled glass of

whiskey. 'I think the real question is: are you?'

The grin he'd grown familiar with over the years crossed her face and he knew they could go back to the friendship they'd once had, after all. Her eyes dropped to the glass he held. 'I thought you don't drink whiskey,' she said.

'I don't,' he replied, downing the amber liquid again.

She laughed as he took her hand and led her to the dancefloor. They fell into step, dancing around Scott and Olivia, Chad and Vanessa doing the same. As they turned, he caught a glimpse of Betty kissing her date. He swallowed the lump in his throat and tore his gaze away from them. What he'd had with Liz was fun, and Betty may have been a rebound at first, but what he'd had with her was special. And she threw it away for another man.

'Is that her?' Liz asked, trying to see what he was looking at.

He looked at her questioningly. 'How do you—'

'Oliva told me,' she replied. 'She said she wouldn't have invited her if she hadn't been doing the flowers. She wasn't supposed to bring a date, though. I'm sorry it didn't work out for you, Alex.'

The song changed, and more people joined them on the dancefloor. He shook his head. 'It doesn't matter,' he said. 'I'll never have to see her again.'

She pulled back, searching his eyes. 'Why is that?'

'Because, this time tomorrow, I'll be standing in front of my new home in Ireland.'

She didn't seem to understand, so he led her off

the dancefloor, pulled out the papers from his pocket, and showed them to her.

'Kinsale?' she said, her eyes scanning the papers.

'In good ol' County Cork,' he said, smiling. She laughed.

'County Cork?' she said. 'I can't imagine you living anywhere outside of a city.'

'Well, prepare to be amazed,' he said, feeling a temporary moment of relief at the light-heartedness in which they could joke.

'So, what does this all mean?' she asked, handing the papers back to him.

'It means I'm the new owner of an inn, *The Irish Maiden*, courtesy of my deceased great uncle.'

'Your *great uncle*?'

He shrugged. 'He married my grandmother's sister. They never had children and I'm apparently the only relative he had that's still alive.'

'Does Scott know?'

He nodded. 'I told him and Olivia last night.'

'Well, Mr Carter,' she said in her best Irish accent, her grin slightly higher on her left side, but her eyes saddened. 'I hope you find happiness in Ireland.'

So did he, but he wasn't getting his hopes up.

At least it would be a distraction.

Chapter 1

Alex stared at the building in front of him, reading the faded letters on the sign—*The Irish Maiden*. He looked back down at the worn piece of paper he held in his hand, rechecking the address, hoping there would be another inn called *The Irish Maiden* in Kinsale. He had the right address—this was it. He sighed, looking back at the building which looked rather worse for wear.

The wooden porch was caving in where the wood was rotting. One of the posts holding up the veranda had snapped in half, pulling the corner of the veranda down with it. The windows upstairs were grimy, and there were patches of board covering up holes in the walls. It looked as though it hadn't had a fresh coat of paint in years—probably forty years or so if Alex had his guess.

Inside, the inn wasn't much better. The front door creaked, almost wobbling off its hinges. He faced the front desk—it, at least, looked organised—then took in the rest of the room. The dining tables, all mismatched, were set to his left—he was surprised to see a few people sitting there, eating—and there were lounge chairs and sofas to his right with smouldering embers in the fireplace in the corner and a staircase between the lounge area and the front desk.

It looked as though there wasn't much order. He shuddered to think of what upstairs would look like. Every picture on the walls was crooked except for an old photograph of two young men standing in front of the inn—it looked good then—that was hanging behind the front desk. He assumed one of the men was his great uncle, Carrick Fitzpatrick, but he had no idea who the other was.

How was this place still running? And why hadn't Carrick ever renovated the inn or, at least, maintained it? He couldn't imagine the inn getting too busy in a small fishing town like Kinsale. Though, he did spy some people who looked like tourists admiring the brightly coloured shop-fronts on the main street. But who would venture to the edge of town to stay in an inn that could very well collapse on top of them?

Maybe he should have simply told the attorney he didn't want the inn—that would have been the easier route to take. But he needed a distraction to get his mind off Betty, and diving into a project as big as fixing up this ramshackle inn could just do the trick. Besides, he'd put too much effort into getting a work visa and striking a deal to gain citizenship to back out now.

One year. That's all he had. One year from the start of his visa and one condition to gain citizenship—turn *The Irish Maiden* into a successful business. He started wishing he'd come to Kinsale the second he got his visa instead of waiting out for two months because Betty was hesitant about coming with him. Looking back on it now, he knew why she was hesitant—she was seeing someone on the side.

Maybe he would have come straight away, had he known how much work the inn would need on it just to get it up to standard. But then, maybe he wouldn't have come at all if he knew what state it was in. On the other hand, he needed a new beginning. And this inn was the perfect excuse.

He took off his suit jacket, feeling grossly over-dressed, and found some paper and a pen behind the front desk to start writing a list of things that needed to be done. He had ten months to make this place successful or he would be kicked out of the country. He figured he would need months to fix it up before he could even think about making it successful— especially since he would have to do it all himself with limited funds. It would be an impossible task, but at least it would keep him busy for the next ten months.

Alex startled as a door near the dining room burst open and a stocky, bald man—just over five-foot tall and looked to be in his late sixties—who was mid-conversation with a tall, lanky, younger man—probably in his early twenties—came out, carrying some bowls to the people sitting at the tables. The aroma drifted from the kitchen and hit Alex—lamb stew. He recognised the smell from Scott's parent's place in Australia. Suzie Henders always liked making lamb stew, and he and Scott always liked eating it.

When the two men turned to head back towards the kitchen, the older man halted briefly before bee-lining towards Alex.

'Aye, yer not s'posed to be behind there,' he said, his accent thick. He tapped on the front desk. 'Staff only.'

'Then, I think I'm well within my rights to be here,' Alex replied.

Judging by the look on the older man's face and the steam he could practically see fuming out of his ears, he figured the man really had no idea who he was.

'My apologies,' he said quickly. 'I gather the attorney didn't tell you I was coming.'

'The attorney?' His face started to soften. 'Aye, he called. Said to expect a Mr Carter.'

Alex extended his hand. 'Please, just call me Alex.'

'Ailbe O'Connor,' he said, shaking Alex's hand. 'Or Al, for short.' He patted the younger man on the shoulder. 'And this 'ere young lad is Lee Campbell, so named because he was conceived near the River Lee. He brings in the deliveries.'

Alex thought he could see Lee's cheeks tinge red from the comment. He shook his hand and looked back at Al. 'So, I assume you're the inn keeper?'

Al nodded. 'And everythin' else 'round 'ere.'

'So, you're who I need to talk to about fixing this place up, then.'

Al's face grew solemn and he scratched his chin. 'Aye, straight to business. Was hopin' we might get a lad like ye. Wasn't expecting ye to be so—'

'Young?' Alex replied.

Al shook his head. 'Nay,' he said. 'Eager. Not once ye seen the place, anyway.'

Alex straightened up. He didn't feel very eager once he had realised how run down the inn was. But what better time to start than now? Al sent Lee on his way, reminding him to bring garlic next time, and led Alex to his office—if it could really be called that. It was a tiny room with a small desk in the middle of it pushed right against one wall with a gap of about a foot between it and the other wall. There were papers piled high over the top and a single chair on the other side. He was surprised the door could even be opened, though it did bump against the desk if you tried to open it further.

Al squeezed between the wall and the desk and sat in the chair. It was a rather funny sight—it looked as though it had been pushed right up against him, pinning him to the wall. He spread his arms out over the desk, a proud look on his face.

'This is me office,' he said. Then, his face dropped. 'Though, I s'pose it's yers now, being the new owner and all.'

'Is this a broom cupboard?' Alex asked, not sure if he could wipe the surprise from his face.

Al frowned. 'Nay, it's me office. I just told ye that.' He scratched his chin. 'But the broom cupboard? Aye, that would have more room.' He pointed to Alex. 'Tell ye what, *ye* can have the broom cupboard and I'll keep me office.'

A smile twitched on Alex's face. This man was quite the character—he was sure they would get along well enough. He wondered how big the broom cupboard was, but decided it shouldn't matter. He didn't really need an office—not while he was fixing up the place, anyway. Maybe he could factor a bigger office into his renovations, maybe even make Al's office bigger. He reached his hand over the desk.

'Deal.'

Al paused for a second before shaking Alex's hand enthusiastically. 'Yer a good lad, Mr Carter.'

'You *can* call me Alex,' he reminded him.

'Nay,' Al said, shaking his head. 'I couldn't be calling ye that, Mr Carter. A good lad like ye should be shown some respect.'

Alex smiled, leaning against the wall. He was starting to like Al. Though, he wasn't too sure about being called Mr Carter. Al would be the only person to have ever addressed him that way. But then again, maybe he could get used to it.

'To business then,' Al said, shifting himself in the

chair as if to get more comfortable but looking even less so. 'I hope ye got some business degree or somethin', ye'll need it.'

'I'm a painter by trade,' Alex replied. The thought of needing any kind of business experience hadn't even crossed his mind.

Al studied Alex and sighed. 'Well,' he said. 'At least that'll come in handy 'ere.'

Alex nodded, hesitating before asking the question he had been pondering. 'Al,' he started. 'How come this place hasn't already been renovated or, at the very least, maintained?'

Al's eyes grew solemn and he picked at a flake of wood on his desk. 'Yer uncle wasn't much into fixing up a place that was never very successful. He struggled for a long time with his health, always knackered. Never had no time to work on it. Probably why this place is in tatters.'

He examined the flake of wood between his fingers before flicking it onto the floor. Alex stared at the speck of raw, worn wood where the flake was.

'I suppose you never had time to work on it, either?' he asked, hesitantly.

Al's eyes shot up towards Alex, his brow furrowed. 'I was a lookin' after Mr Fitzpatrick 'til the day he died,' he said. 'Had to let go of most of the staff 'cause he couldn't afford to pay 'em, so I had to do more than me fair share of work 'round 'ere. But no use in olagonin'—I owed him one.' He paused briefly, and Alex thought he could see a tear threatening to spill. 'Ye know, me daddy was right there beside him when he opened this place. And he was right there with me daddy when he breathed his last breath.'

'I'm sorry,' Alex said. He didn't know what else he could say. But now he knew who the other young man in the photograph was.

***

Infuriated. That's what she was. Infuriated, exasperated, and at her wit's end. And to think she wanted him to own up to his indiscretions. Brigid revved the engine of her car, tearing out onto the street while Darcy chased after her to the end of the driveway yelling obscenities. She ignored the speculating glances of his neighbours. They would all say she asked for it. Nothing was ever Darcy Flannigan's fault.

Darcy Flannigan—a sorry excuse of a man and her arrogant jerk of a boyfriend or, should she say, *ex*-boyfriend. She tilted her head. Was he even her ex-boyfriend if he was convinced they were nothing exclusive and found it well within his rights to date and propose to someone else while they had been together? He'd gotten her drunk, said all the right things, and slept with her. And she was stupid enough to believe everything he said. It was a night that made her sick to the bone and she regretted it more than anything. But she would never be able to forget it. Not when she would have a reminder of it every day for the rest of her life.

She clutched her stomach and swallowed. How could she be so foolish? She only started seeing Darcy because her father had been practically pushing him onto her and she wanted her father to be proud of her for once. And she only went to Darcy's house now because she had no other choice. She'd suggested they marry—worst idea ever.

'What made you think I was ever going to marry you?' he had said.

His words had hurt. But she should have been more guarded from the start. Someone who worked at a tattered inn had no chance with Darcy Flannigan, even if she were that way inclined. Which she wasn't. Not anymore. Darcy Flannigan was the last person on earth she would ever want to be with now.

Her father would be disappointed. *Her father*. He was respected by each and every person in this whole area. But their relationship has been like walking on ice since her mother died. Not even her sister, Colleen, had been able to be a buffer for her at the best of times. She shook her head. He would be disappointed in *her*. He already felt ashamed of her for working in such an unkempt place as *The Irish Maiden*, he would cast her out if he knew. She pulled her car to a stop outside the inn she'd grown to love, touching her hand to her stomach again.

It was only a matter of time before he found out.

Chapter 2

'Ailbe!' Brigid yelled, storming through the front door of the inn and leaving the door to close itself. 'Ailbe!'

She pushed through to the kitchen, spinning on her heel to find he wasn't there and went back out to the front room. Where the hell was he? How could she vent to him if he couldn't be found? She called for him once more, drawing out the syllables of his name, and jumped when she heard his voice behind her.

'What be goin' on out here, wee lass?'

She turned to face him, pointing her finger at him. 'You were right,' she said. 'Darcy *is* a jerk! Though, I believe you said he's nothing but a shaper and a chancer.'

'Aye,' he said, scratching his chin. 'I did say that.'

'And you were *right*,' she repeated, slamming her open palm onto the front desk. 'He's a … a …'

'Ponce?' Al offered.

She shook her head. 'No, that doesn't really fit the bill.' She paused, then waved her finger in front of her again. 'Actually, I would call him anything right now. So, yes, he is a ponce. And he's an idiot. A stupid, stupid idiot. You know what else he is, Ailbe?' she continued before Al could do more than shake his head. 'He's a pathetic, lying, two-faced, cheating *bastard*!'

Al put his hands up in front of him. 'Oh, now, a lovely lass like ye shouldn't be usin' that kind of language,' he said, tilting his head to the side.

'But he *is*, Ailbe. He. Is. A. Bastard,' she said, resting her head on her arms on the desk. 'I can't believe Daddy likes him.'

Ailbe rubbed his hand on her back. 'Well, like ye said, he's two-faced.'

'Well, he was wrong, and you were right, Ailbe,' she said into her arms. 'And now Daddy will cast me out because of *him*.'

She sobbed into her arms. Her father *would* cast her out if he knew, even though it was really his fault for practically throwing her at Darcy in the first place. She'd never liked Darcy to start with—she always saw him for what he really was. But after her father had put so much pressure on her to be with him, she'd started to wonder if she had been judging a book by its cover. And he'd had her fooled. Like she said, he was two-faced.

'Ye never said what ye were fighting about, lass,' Al said gently. 'And why would yer daddy cast ye out?'

She stayed silent. She knew she shouldn't have mentioned that last part, but Ailbe had a way of making her feel safe. He'd always reminded her that she was like a daughter to him, and she knew he was always a better father to her than her own was. Al patted her back.

'Ye don't need to tell me,' he said softly. 'But I know yer daddy, and there's only one thing that would make him cast ye out of yer own home, and that's if yer plugged.'

She still didn't answer but lifted her chin up to face him. He smiled at her and pressed his hand to her cheek.

'But if ye found yerself without a place to call home,' he continued. 'Ye can always stay with me.'

She forced a smile. 'Thank you, Ailbe,' she whispered. 'I'll see how I go.'

His smile broadened. 'There's me lass,' he said.

She watched him walk back to his office and sighed as the door closed. It wouldn't be that easy— and she wouldn't want to burden Al with looking after her and her baby. She had to come up with another plan. She picked up a pen and tapped it against the desk, only to drop it on the floor when the front door swung open.

***

'Sorry about that, Mr Carter,' Al said, sliding himself back behind the desk. 'It was just the wee lass that works here. She's having some … err, troubles. She's always been like blood to me.'

Alex nodded, and they started looking at plans to fix up the inn again. *Wee lass*. He wasn't one to eavesdrop, but it was hard not to hear them with the office door left open. And, in his experience, a voice that has a ring to it like hers does, despite being filled with anger and using so many colourful adjectives to describe someone, doesn't usually belong to a *wee lass*, but to a fiery, independent, usually attractive, educated woman. He'd managed to stop himself from poking his head out the door to put a face to the voice. Whoever this Darcy was, she was obviously involved with him—even if she didn't seem very happy about it.

But why should that matter? He wasn't in Kinsale to look for a relationship. After what happened with Betty, he figured he wouldn't be jumping into anything so quickly again. He was here for two things—a distraction, and to make *The Irish Maiden* successful. But the distraction couldn't interfere with making the inn successful. Their discussion was interrupted again by a *thud* and her voice yelling.

'Let me go!'

Before Alex knew it, he was out the office door and headed towards the ruckus, his heart beating fast and everything slowing down around him. A man—Darcy, he presumed—had her pinned against the wall, his finger pressed to her stomach.

'You *will* get rid of it!' Darcy said.

She struggled against his grip. 'You're mad if you think I'll do anything you say!'

'I'm warning you Brigid,' he said, snarling. 'Get rid of it, or I'll get rid of it for you.'

'What are you going to do, Darcy?' she spat back at him. 'Force me again? Just so *she* doesn't find out?'

He pressed her harder against the wall, and Alex found himself moving quicker.

'You heard her, asshole,' Alex said, his blood heating. 'Back off.'

Darcy softened his grip, turning slightly to face Alex, his face maddened as he looked him up and down. 'How about you keep your nose out of matters that don't concern you, *pretty boy*.'

Pretty boy? Alex clenched his jaw. Sure, he'd rocked up in a suit—grossly overdressed for the less than casual standard of this inn—but nobody called him a pretty boy. As he moved closer, he saw Brigid's heel come down hard on Darcy's foot. Darcy swore and swung his arm at her, colliding with Alex's jaw instead. How had he managed to put himself between them so quickly? He followed Darcy's punch with a solid one of his own, feeling the crunch of Darcy's nose against his fist. He rubbed his jaw as he watched Darcy stagger backwards, his hand held to his nose and covered in blood.

'Get out of here, Darcy,' Al said, his voice firm. 'Or I'll be calling the Garda and yer daddy won't be happy about that.'

Darcy seemed to consider the situation briefly, then waved his free hand, pointing to Brigid, before leaving. 'Remember what I said, Brigid.'

Alex waited until Darcy was out the door before speaking. 'Are you okay?' he asked, turning to face Brigid, and feeling as though the wind was knocked out of him.

Her eyes. If green eyes could be described as fiery, hers would be the textbook example. They were a deep green—a few shades darker than emerald—standing out against her porcelain skin like the moss on a white rock he'd admired as a child. Her skin was flawless, even with a few freckles splashed across the bridge of her perfectly straight nose. Her long auburn hair fell in gentle waves over her slender shoulders and her supple lips looked like soft velvet against perfection.

'I had it under control.'

And there was the punch that reminded him to breathe. 'Oh, it looked like it,' he retorted.

She scowled at him. 'Well,' she pursed her lips together. 'You didn't have to break his nose.'

'He tried to *hit* you, Brigid!'

She jerked her head back. 'Oh, I'm sorry, I don't recall telling you my name,' she said sarcastically. 'And you are?'

'Alex.'

'Well, Alex,' she continued. 'I don't need your help. I can look after myself.' She turned and started to walk towards the kitchen.

'Are you really pregnant?' he asked, wondering

why he even had to know.

She spun on her heel, storming towards him and pressing her finger against his chest. 'You know, Darcy was right—you *should* stay out of matters that don't concern you. Who do you think you are, anyway? You can't just go around asking questions like you own the place.'

He raised an eyebrow, staring into those green eyes that weren't just fiery now, they were wild. He could feel the sparks shooting through her fingertip into his chest—a feeling he'd never felt before, not even with Betty. But despite that, he could feel his own blood boiling. Who did he think he was? He just took a blow that was meant for her and got her out of the way of a bastard who obviously wouldn't think twice about hitting a woman. The least she could do is thank him. He was about to tell her he *did* own the place, that he was now her boss and that she should really thank someone who helps her whether she wanted it or not, but found it was too late. Her eyes grew wider and she started shaking her head.

'Oh, you have got to be kidding me,' she said, glancing over to Al. 'This is him? This is Mr Fitzpatrick's nephew?' Al nodded.

'Great nephew,' Alex corrected.

'I don't care who you are, I'm not working for you,' she snapped and started walking towards the door. 'Ailbe, can I talk to you, please?'

Alex clenched his jaw, rubbing it where it still ached. Had a woman ever made him so infuriated and irritated in his life as this one managed to do in a few minutes? Not only had she been ungrateful, she'd been straight-up rude. And why was she mad at him? He took a punch for her. He picked the pen up off the floor and fiddled with it before tucking it into his pocket. His blood was boiling. She wouldn't work for him? Maybe that was a good thing. She made him feel furious, frustrated, and stupid.

But God, she was the most beautiful and enchanting creature he'd ever laid eyes on.

***

'What's goin' on, lass?' Al said as he closed the door behind him.

She closed her eyes for a second, then turned to face him. 'Why didn't you tell me he was in there with you, Ailbe?' she asked.

'He wanted to get straight to business. I know we weren't expecting him,' Al said. 'But ye can't be talking to Mr Carter like that. He could have yer job. That is, if yer not already leavin' me.'

Brigid sighed. 'I didn't say I was leaving,' she said. 'I said I'm not working for him.'

'Well, that's the same thing, lass,' Al said, taking hold of her arms. 'He owns this place now, so we work for him.'

'Why didn't Mr Fitzpatrick leave the inn to you, Ailbe?' she asked, pouting. 'It only seemed the fair thing to do since your daddy helped him start it and you put your life into looking after him and this place.'

'He wanted to keep it in the family,' he said, shrugging. 'Mr Carter is his only living kin. Besides, I'm too old to be taking on an inn.' He patted her on her arm and turned to head back inside. 'Ye remember me offer, lass. I'm not too old to be looking after ye and yer babe.'

She felt a tear threatening while she watched Al head back inside and sighed as the door closed. She didn't know why she was so rude to Alex. He was tall, dark, and handsome, after all. And incredibly attractive, especially since he had punched Darcy for trying to hurt her when he hadn't even met her yet. She smiled at the new memory of seeing Darcy holding his broken nose. But even though the sentiment warmed her, she wished he hadn't become involved with this.

She knew his type and she despised that kind of character. The high-class businessman who flies in from another country to take over a failing business, fix it up, and sell it to the highest bidder. A man who hasn't worked a single day of hard labour in his life and thinks he can have anything he wants at the drop of a hat. He's easy to fall for and demands respect from his employees. But he wouldn't get it from her.

She could see the fire in his eyes when he told Darcy to back off. She could see his body stiffen when she told him to mind his own business, and his arrogance in correcting her. She felt the shock of electricity when her finger touched his chest. She saw the intensity in his gaze when they connected eyes. She'd felt it down to her core. Like her, his eyes were green—though darker; almost a blue. His hair was as black as the dead of night and she'd wanted to see if it felt as silky as it looked. His skin was slightly tanned, and she had seen the vein on the side of his neck pulsing quicker than it should.

He looked exactly like someone she would fall for, and she'd freaked. That's why she had been so rude to him. When he'd finished what he came here to do, he would leave, leaving her behind. And it would be just as well. She touched her hand to her stomach. She had someone else she had to think about now. She couldn't be selfish in wanting anything.

Chapter 3

Alex wiped the sweat from his brow. Despite the cooler temperatures in Kinsale than what he was used to, working hard still made his body temperature shoot through the roof. He unbuttoned his shirt, letting the cool breeze catch and cool his body. He may have been overdressed yesterday, but the paint-stained jeans, green flannelette shirt, dark blue singlet, and work boots made him feel a little underdressed—especially since everyone he saw was wearing a jacket outside, including Lee, who he'd recruited to help him out.

He held the post that Lee was bolting into place upright. They'd made good time. Soon, they would have this post in place and the veranda repaired. He'd started with replacing the floorboards of the veranda at the crack of dawn, surprised at how fast he could work when he was focussed on forgetting. They still had plenty of work to do outside— replacing windows and some of the weatherboards. The whole thing had to be repainted. Then there was the garden, but that would be the last thing on his agenda.

Inside had a lot more to do. Doors had to be replaced, the floors had to be redone, holes patched up and a fresh coat of paint throughout. He hadn't had the chance to have a look at all the rooms yet, but the room he was staying in certainly needed a good deal of work. If he could find the money, maybe he could organise some kind of heating for the rooms as well. He looked around, putting together his plan of attack. The next thing on his agenda was to replace the damn front door that kept creaking with the wind. Maybe find one that locks.

'How are you going up there, mate?' he said.

Lee rested his hands on the gutter. 'I think this should do it. As long as we don't have anyone slammed against it again, we should be all right.'

'Is that how it broke to begin with?'

Lee nodded, climbing down the ladder. 'Drunken fight between two guys. Over a woman, I think. Pat was half the size of Pete, but he could move—he had that on him.'

'Does that happen often?'

'Fights?' Lee shrugged, wobbling his head from side to side. 'Only most nights. They do it for a *craic*. They'll be best pals the next day.'

'Well, let's hope this post stays put for a while.' He figured it should be able to take a beating. It looked steady enough.

Alex felt his stomach rumble and figured it must be close to lunchtime. He hadn't seen Brigid all morning. Not that he was working outside in hopes he might see her. He may find her infuriating, but there was something about her that made it so he couldn't stop thinking about her—thinking about running his fingers through her long auburn hair, wondering if her skin felt like the porcelain it looked like or if it was soft and rich, if her lips tasted as velvety as they looked, how her body felt beneath his hands …

'I'll bet Al has something ready for us to eat,' Lee said, leading the way back into the inn.

When Alex got to the door, he gave it a little shake to size it up, lifting it off it's hinges. He cursed as the lower panel of the door fell off, and he took it outside, throwing it onto the pile of rubbish. The door had come off much easier than he'd anticipated, and it was definitely beyond repair. He'd have to replace it as soon as he could. By the time he was back inside, taking a seat at the table with Lee, Ailbe was staring at the empty space where the door used to be.

'Where's me door?' Ailbe said.

'It's gone, Al,' he said, patting the older man on the shoulder.

Al's lip quivered. 'But I liked that door.'

'It's not coming back,' Alex said.

Ailbe shrugged, heading back to the kitchen. 'Yer the boss, Mr Carter.'

Alex started eating the stew, or savouring, more like it. It reminded him of home—home with Scott, Suzie and Rob, and Liz, the only family he ever really knew. But there was something in Ailbe's tone that had him agitated.

'Is he all right?' he said.

'I think he's just worried about Brigid,' Lee said. 'He's always had a soft spot for her. Always wants the best for her.'

'What's her story, anyway?' he said, trying to sound disinterested. Lee raised an eyebrow, his spoon stopping halfway between his bowl and his mouth. 'I'm just trying to find out a little about my … employees.' It felt strange calling her that. Honestly, it seemed like she had more run of the place than he did.

Lee hesitated, as if considering Alex for a while, before clearing his throat. 'Brigid comes from a strict family. Her daddy is on the council, so he's very respected. The Murphy family goes right back to one of the founders of Kinsale. I guess you could say he has an honorary position, and he owns the fishing industry for the area. He's a good man, but very ground in tradition—especially when it comes to Brigid and Colleen.'

'Colleen?'

'Brigid's younger sister,' Lee explained.

'What about her mother?'

Lee shook his head. 'Her mammy died when

Brigid was sixteen. Her daddy's put a lot of pressure on her since then. Ridiculous if you ask me, but who am I to say anything?'

Alex spooned some more of the stew into his mouth. If Brigid really were pregnant, then she did have a predicament with her living situation. He'd overheard the conversation yesterday between her and Ailbe. The part where she said her daddy would cast her out had him thinking she was exaggerating. But now, he realised that maybe she wasn't. He couldn't stop the thoughts accumulating in his mind—plans. For him, for this inn. For Brigid. If he ever saw her again.

'Do you have plans for Wednesday night, Alex?'

Lee's question snapped him out of his thoughts. He was relieved Lee had agreed to call him Alex instead of Mr Carter. Though Ailbe was still determined to keep with the whole Mr Carter thing, he still couldn't get used to the idea of anyone else calling him that.

Alex shrugged. What plans would he have? He'd only been living here for a total of … well … one night. 'Probably doing as much work as I can around here,' he said.

Of course, the more work he did, the more it would keep his mind off things. Off Brigid. He lifted his eyes from staring at the food, but not necessarily looking at anything. When had his mind switched from distracting himself from thinking about Betty, to thinking about Brigid? The thought had come so easily. Too easily. It scared him.

Lee shook his head. 'Tell you what, come over for dinner,' he said. 'Moira's cooking her famous roast. Call it a welcoming gift from us, to you.'

'Well, I—' He was inviting him over for dinner with his family? The only other place he'd had that with was with Scott's family. 'That makes my plans seem very mundane. So, thank you. I'd love to come.'

Lee smiled, and he wondered if he had many friends. He knew of people who'd struggled to make friends once they were married, and even more so when kids came along. He knew Lee had a daughter, and that he worked at his family's business—*The Hound & The Harp*, one of the local pubs. Surely, he wouldn't have much time for socialising.

'Good,' he said. 'Moira will be excited. She loves having people over for dinner.'

They finished off their stew, Ailbe coming over right as he put his spoon in the bowl. He dropped an envelope on the table in front of Alex. 'That there's a … ahh … small fortune Mr Fitzpatrick left for ye. Had to find the details, but it's all there.'

Alex opened the envelope, pulling out a bank statement, what looked like the paperwork for it to be transferred into Alex's name, and the details to access it in the meantime. His eyes scanned to the balance, his mouth dropping open. *Small fortune?* That amount of money would turn this ramshackle inn into a freaking mansion! He looked up at Ailbe, who only winked at him and turned to head back towards the kitchen.

'Fix me damn door!' he called over his shoulder.

Fix the door? With that *small fortune*, Alex could replace the damn door with a door made of gold and have some leftover.

Shoot. Maybe this project wouldn't be as hard as he'd thought it would be.

***

Brigid stared at the tones of purple and yellow appearing on her forearm. She knew Darcy had pinned her to the wall quite roughly, but to actually form a bruise? Maybe it was the adrenaline and anger coursing through her veins while she was pinned that made her not realise he was hurting her. She still couldn't believe he was going to hit her, and Alex took the blow without even knowing her

'What's that?'

She yanked her sleeve over the bruise, wincing as her hand bumped against it, and looked up at her younger sister. She hadn't realised her door was ajar, or even thought it might have mattered—until she'd noticed the bruise.

'It's nothing,' she mumbled, swinging her legs off the bed, and grabbing her jacket.

She'd slept in, then got distracted with the bruise for so long she was running late for work. Not that it *really* mattered what time she showed up, as long as she put in the hours. Well, it never mattered with Ailbe running the inn. She didn't know how it would be with Alex. She pushed her arm through the jacket sleeve, but Colleen was quick, pushing the sleeve up to see the bruise as soon as her arm was through.

'*This* isn't nothing, Brigid,' she said, holding her arm up so she could see the bruise again. Like she needed to see the bruise again. Every movement that twinged those muscles made it ache. Colleen leaned closer. 'Did Darcy do this?'

Brigid squinted, freeing her arm from her sister and adjusting her jacket. 'What do *you* think?'

Colleen sat on Brigid's bed. 'I think he's a two-faced arrogant bastard.' Brigid smiled. Colleen had secretly taken on her colourful language after all. But she'd never let their daddy hear it. 'I heard about their engagement.'

Brigid sighed. 'Yeah, well, that's not what we were fighting about.' She lowered her voice, as if mumbling to herself. 'Not entirely, anyway.' She pulled her boots on.

'I thought you wouldn't have let him off scot free for cheating on you like that,' Colleen said, her brow furrowed.

'I didn't know about that,' Brigid scoffed. 'At least not when I approached him to suggest we get married.'

'*Married?*' Colleen's mouth dropped open. 'You've never really liked the guy! Why would you—'

Brigid raised an eyebrow. She knew she was giving away too much information. But she also knew Colleen wasn't just her sister, but she was also her best friend who knew everything about her. She wouldn't have been able to keep it a secret from her if she tried.

'Brigid.' Colleen lowered her voice to a whisper. 'You're not … pregnant … are you?'

Brigid cringed.

'Oh. My. G—' Brigid clamped her hand over Colleen's mouth.

'Colleen, please. Daddy will hear you.' She released Colleen and let out a sigh. 'I don't know for certain, but I'm late.'

'How late?'

'Like, a month late.' Give or take.

'You have to tell him, Brigid,' Colleen said, taking hold of Brigid's hand.

She appreciated the gesture, but she didn't need comforting. That was her job as the older sister. She had to be strong for Colleen. She always had been. 'He can't know,' she said flatly.

'He's going to find out when you start showing.'

'I'll figure something out before then.'

She had no idea what exactly that would be. But her prospects were looking like she'd be raising the baby on her own. She wondered if Daddy would let her still see Colleen when he disowned her. She hated that her daddy was so set in traditional beliefs. It was the twenty-first century, after all. People got pregnant outside of marriage all the time. But in her family …

'Like what?'

She looked into Colleen's eyes. Her eyes were a hazy brown, matching the chestnut of her hair. Brigid had been the one lucky enough to look like their mother, inheriting her green eyes and auburn hair. Colleen took after their daddy, even though she'd deny it. She gave Colleen's hand a squeeze before letting it go.

'I don't know,' she said. 'I guess I'll have to leave before he finds out.' She swept a kiss onto her sister's cheek. 'Now, let me get to work, will you? I'm late.' Colleen let out something that sounded somewhere between a laugh and a snort. Brigid rolled her eyes. 'Oh, shush you.'

On one hand, she was relieved Colleen knew. But on the other ... she knew it was only a matter of time before her daddy found out, and she didn't want Colleen to be the one put under pressure to tell him. She had to work something out. Something that would be believable, that she could convince her daddy that it wasn't what it ... well ... was.

By the time she got to work, she felt like she needed the distraction—anything to keep her mind off her situation and her impending doom. And, for a moment, that tall handsome chunk of muscle fixing the railing on the veranda was a good distraction. Until he turned to face her.

Shoot.

Alex faced her front on as she walked towards the inn, one hand wiping his forehead, the other hand on his hip, perfectly pushing his shirt to the side enough for her to see his dark blue singlet hugging his body in all the right places. She'd thought he must be strong to have knocked Darcy to the floor with one hit, but *damn*. Who knew suits could hide a body made of boulders so neatly?

'So, you decided to show after all.' It was more a statement than a question.

She felt her cheeks flush and wondered how much like a tomato she looked. That was the problem with fair skin—a blush was impossible to hide. She tried to think of something witty to say, something to realign her thoughts. He was her *boss*, after all. And he wouldn't be one to hang around regardless of how much he might say it. She knew the fate of the inn. She'd seen it happen with all the other businesses in town that got passed on to family members. But then, she'd never seen any of those people getting their hands dirty with repairing the places themselves. Maybe Alex was different, but she couldn't think about that. She could be raising Darcy's baby. No one would want to take that on.

She hadn't realised he'd fallen into step next to her until she'd reached the door, putting her hand out and touching … nothing?

'Where's the door?' she said, blinking her eyes, and realising she probably sounded more stupid than witty. She heard a chuckle next to her and shot her eyes towards him.

'Who needs one?' he said, spreading his arms out to emphasise his point. 'I thought we'd try an open-door policy. What do you think?'

'I think you're mad.'

***

Priceless.

He would give anything to see that look on her face again. There was a mixture of shock, surprise, fury. She squinted at him, which only made his body shake more. It wouldn't take much to send him into full-blown laughter. She pointed inside the inn.

'You *need* a door, otherwise it'll be freaking freezing in here!'

That would do it. His laugh sounded more of a rumble, and he was certain his tone had *flirt* written all over it, even if he tried to avoid it. He didn't know why he found it so fascinating to be teasing Brigid like that. But she made him feel something, right down to his core, and it was something he hadn't felt for a long time. Or ever, if he thought about it. Even with her brow creased and her eyes wild, all he wanted to do was see her smile. He was yet to see that elusive smile, but he had a feeling it would be the end of him. Maybe the feelings were real. Or maybe it was pure lust, and his mind running wild with ideas he knew only had a slim chance of being followed through. Whatever it was, there was something about her that made him want her—need her, even.

He hadn't wanted to start a relationship when he moved to Kinsale. But there was also no point in being celibate for as long as he was here. In saying that, he thought he might be happy enough if he was to stay there permanently. He liked the people, the work, the distance. It really could be the long-term change he needed. If he could just find a way to make the inn work for him …

'What are you laughing at?' she said, placing her hands on her hips.

'Just your expression,' he said, shrugging. His laughter had settled, but he couldn't wipe the smile from his face. She shook her head questioningly. 'I was joking, Brigid. The door will be replaced by the end of the day.'

She frowned at him, then spun on her heel. 'Good.'

That was it? That's all she had to say? Not even a smile? Maybe getting that smile would be harder than he thought. He followed her to the front desk and watched as she searched all over the bench and through the drawers.

'Damn it!' She slapped her hand on the bench, then glared at him. 'Do you need something?'

He raised an eyebrow and leaned against the desk. 'What are you looking for?'

'Not that it should concern you,' she said. 'But my pen.'

'You don't have another?' He thought a business might have more than one pen available.

She sighed. 'No, I do not have another pen.' At first, he'd thought she was being sarcastic, but when she placed both hands on the desk and leaned forward a little, her head bowed, he realised she was serious. 'They keep going missing until there's only one left. I had it yesterday when—' she broke off, not finishing her sentence. But she didn't have to.

Alex reached into his shirt pocket and pulled the

pen out, handing it to her. 'Here,' he said, nudging her arm with his. 'I picked it up off the floor yesterday.'

She took the pen, her eyes granting him a flash of gratefulness before her tone turned witty again. 'You didn't think to just put it on the desk?'

He leaned towards her. He could smell the sweetness of her perfume and the mint in her breath. It was alluring. Divine. Almost too much. 'What kind of a business only has one pen?'

Then he saw it. A smile. Well, almost. Her lip curved slightly to one side, and, for a moment, his heart stopped. She leaned closer towards him. Her lips were only a few inches away from his. He could close that distance with little effort.

'Well, Mr Carter,' she said. 'Perhaps you should take that up with the boss.'

Then she pulled away. He felt a rumble at the base of his throat. He hadn't wanted anyone calling him that—he'd made the exception of Ailbe—but God, it sounded so much sexier coming from her lips. Then, he didn't register the words coming from his mouth.

'So, it seems you're in quite the predicament, Brigid.'

She spun towards him, her eyes wide. He'd already said it, he couldn't stop now. 'What did you say?' Her tone had a hint of warning in it.

He shrugged, folding his arms across his chest. 'You know, I'm sure your condition wouldn't go down too well with your daddy, especially with him being so respected and traditional.' Where was this coming from? It wasn't like him to act like this. It was almost … blackmail, except he didn't know what for.

She closed the distance between them, her face inches from his again. But this time, she was raging. 'My *condition* is none of your business,' she said. She'd spoken at a whisper, but he could still tell she wasn't happy. 'And I'm not sure I like that you know more about me than I know about you. You don't need to pry to find out more about me, Alex. You should just ask.'

He searched her eyes. They'd softened a little, but she was holding her ground. He wouldn't be surprised if she'd slapped him when he said what he did. God knows, he probably deserved it.

'You wouldn't tell me if I did ask you,' he said.

Her nose crinkled in a way that made him want to smooth it out with his fingers and kiss it back to how it was when she'd almost smiled. But he knew boundaries. And he knew when something would be crossing the line. She nodded her head slowly, turning away from him to busy herself with the pile of paperwork on the edge of the desk.

'You're right. I wouldn't.'

Chapter 4

Wednesday came quicker than he'd thought it would. After his run-in with Brigid on Monday, he'd tried to stay out of her way, which was actually easy enough. Especially since he was working outside from dawn 'til dusk and she left the room or acted busy whenever he came inside. As a peace offering, he'd bought a couple boxes of pens, leaving one on the desk for her and the other in his room for spares. But despite trying to stay out of her way and trying to avoid getting more on her bad side than he already was, his mind refused to cooperate. Brigid featured in his dreams every time he closed his eyes to sleep, sometimes clothed, mostly not. Sometimes only for a moment before he would take her clothes off for her, kissing every inch of her body, feeling the heat radiate to his core as he …

He swore as his hammer came down on his thumb, missing the nail. He couldn't think like this. Not over someone he'd really only just met, knew little about, and who clearly hated his guts. And especially not while he was handling tools that could cause him to lose something if he wasn't careful. He observed his battered thumb, cringing at the sight of blood coming to the surface under his nail. Perhaps now would be a good time for a break.

He leaned against the tree, sipping from his drink bottle, looking at all the work that had been done. They'd almost finished the outside of the building— the veranda was waiting for a coat of varnish on the deck, and the weatherboard was almost fixed up. The only thing that would be left for the outside after today would be a coat of paint and new windows put in upstairs. Though, the windows could wait until he started working on the inside of the rooms. All going well, the painting could be finished tomorrow, Friday at the latest.

He'd appreciated Lee's help. Though he'd expected he might have had to work on a lot of the renovations by himself, Lee had been able to take time off his usual work to help when he could, like for a few hours this morning. Alex squinted at the fancy car that parked in front of the inn, a blue suit climbing out of it, his feet adorned with polished brown shoes. He couldn't resist scoffing at the man. His mother had always said that a man in a blue suit and brown shoes could never be trusted. He wondered if it was just her experience or if it could be passed as a solid fact.

'Ahh, shoot,' he muttered as the man beelined towards him. He recognised the man as the attorney, Julian McCallahan, handling the handover of the inn as he drew closer. 'Afternoon, Julian,' he said as calmly as he could, even though he felt a warning in the pit of his stomach. 'What brings you out here?'

'I thought you might like to hear this in person,' Julian said. 'Shall we step into your office?'

Alex plastered a smile on his face, even though he didn't feel as though it was meant. He spread his arms out. 'You're already in my office, Julian. What's the news?'

'You're not going to like it.'

'Well?'

'You have six months to make this place profitable or you'll be sent out of the country.'

He felt the weight in his chest drop to his stomach. '*Six months*?' he repeated. 'No, that's not right. I still have ten months left. You confirmed that with me on Sunday.'

'I know what I said, but the court has changed the rules.'

'Can they do that?'

'Doesn't matter if they can—they *have*.' Julian rubbed his eyes with his index finger and his thumb. 'They've decided that any foreigners trying to run a business now have six months to make it profitable or they're out of the country. That includes you.' Julian focussed on the inn. 'And by the looks of it, you have your work cut out for you.'

'Six months isn't enough time.'

'There's nothing I can do about it.' Julian tugged at his suit jacket. 'Enjoy the rest of your day, Alex.'

Six months? He'd need a few of those months to fix up this place. The outside was the easy part. There was still so much work to be done to the inside. Then, to make it successful with only a few months remaining? The renovations would be finished in the coldest part of the year when tourist levels were low. He'd be kicked out of the country before the busy season, the inn being sold off to the highest bidder, all the hard work already done for them.

Maybe he should cut his losses now, but he couldn't bring himself to do it. Alex wasn't someone to give up, no matter the costs. And he'd started to grow attached to this place in the few days he'd been here. The people made him feel like a part of the community, even if they were a bit sceptical on the first day. And this inn—it had a charm and character about it that he couldn't let go to waste. Selling it to the highest bidder would be a shame. This was the only part of his family history he had left. This was his roots. And he couldn't let that go without a fight.

'What if I can get citizenship before then?' he asked, putting his hand on the car door to stop Julian from getting in. He hadn't even noticed he had followed after him.

Julian laughed. 'The only way you could get

citizenship in six months is by marrying a reputable local.' His face grew serious. 'But if, perchance, you managed to achieve such a task, the court would leave you alone. If you could gain citizenship, the inn is yours to do with what you want.'

Alex took his hand off the door, a plan forming in his mind. Marriage had always been sacred to him. He only ever wanted to do it the once. But at this point in time, he would do anything to make the most out of the chance given to him for a better life. There must be a reason why his great uncle wanted to keep the inn in the family, passing it on to someone he'd never even met. He wasn't going to give that up. If he could just find a woman willing enough to become his wife …

'If you want my opinion,' Julian said, climbing into the car, and winding the window down to talk to him. 'Quit while you're ahead. You could sell the inn to some locals, pocket the money made, and you'll never have to worry about this building that's better off being hit with a wrecking ball.'

A smile tugged at Alex's lips. He leaned in close, resting his hands on the car. 'Well, it's a good thing I never asked for your opinion, isn't it?'

He pushed off the car, walking back to the inn. The day was drawing to a close, and he had a dinner to go to. Maybe Lee knew of some ideas for the renovations. Alex, on the other hand, could only think about how he was going to find a wife.

***

'Thanks for having me over, Moira,' Brigid said, sipping her non-alcoholic cider. She'd brought her own so no one would suspect anything.

'Honey, you're over almost every week for roast night,' Moira said, pulling the roast out of the oven, the delicious smell wafting through the room. 'There's no need to thank me. You're pretty much expected to be here.'

Other than Colleen, Moira was Brigid's best friend. She could talk to her about things she couldn't talk to Colleen about. If she wanted advice on anything, she could come to her. Usually, between Moira and Lee, they could give some good advice.

'Well, I don't want to get uninvited,' she said. Moira poked her tongue out at her. She glanced over at the table, noticing an extra plate set. 'You know Darcy's not coming, right?' Not that Darcy had come more than once to roast night. The one time he did come, he'd degraded her in front of her friends and made quite a scene. She'd been too embarrassed to bring him again, and she was sure he wouldn't have been welcome anyway.

'Oh, I know,' Moira said, slicing the meat, and putting it onto a serving platter. 'You're better off without him, anyway.'

As if on cue, there was a knock at the door and Aislinn, Lee and Moira's three-year-old daughter, screamed and ran to hide behind the couch. It wasn't unusual for the little girl to do—she did it every time

Brigid visited. But it was the deep voice that spoke that made Brigid's eyes widen and her body stiffen.

'I hope I'm not late.'

'Not at all,' Lee said, his voice chipper.

'This must be him,' Moira whispered, grabbing hold of Brigid's arm, and dragging her into the lounge room, even though she tried digging her heels into the floor so she couldn't be moved.

Him? *Him*? Why was Alex here? Roast night was *their* night! It wasn't invite-your-new-jackass-of-a-boss-to-dinner night! Lee was doing the introductions while Brigid tried to unsuccessfully pry her arm from Moira's grip so she could duck back out to the kitchen.

'This is Aislinn,' he said, placing his hand on her red curls. She mustn't have been hiding for long. 'My wife Moira, and Brigid, who you've already met.'

She faked a smile, but she was sure it looked more of a grimace. She saw a flash in his eyes when they connected with hers across the room. She tore her gaze away and tried to squash the churning feeling in her stomach. He had to have set this up. He *had* to. He must have found out about roast night while he interrogated Lee about her—it had to be Lee, since he'd been spending a lot of time with him and Ailbe certainly wouldn't have given out any information about her—and found a way to get himself invited. If she could just …

'Moira, I think the roast is burning,' she said, widening her eyes at her friend.

A flash of alarm crossed Moira's face before she

squinted. 'No—'

She hoped her eyes looked as pleading as they felt. She had to talk to Moira alone, without looking suspicious. Moira nodded slightly and looked back in the direction of the men.

'Excuse us, please. The roast is calling.' When they got back to the kitchen, Moira spun on her heel to face Brigid. 'What's gotten into you?'

'What's he doing here?' she said, her voice a little over a whisper. Lee and Moira lived in a small house. If they even talked at a normal level, the conversation could be heard from the other room.

Moira shrugged. 'Lee invited him.'

'Why?'

'Because he's new in town.' Moira shook her head. 'Lee's been helping him with the renovations and thought he might be feeling a bit lonely away from his friends and family.'

'Why didn't you tell me?'

'I didn't think it would matter.' She squinted. 'Did you—'

'No, I just—'

'You don't like him?'

Brigid sighed. 'It's not that I don't like him, we just kind of got off to a rough start,' she said. Moira raised an eyebrow. 'I'm just … wary … Moira, I know his type.'

'How do you know his type if you don't even know him?' Moira asked, her expression softening. 'From what Lee's told me, he sounds nice enough. And from what I just witnessed in that room, I think he's interested in you.'

'He's not sticking around,' Brigid said, grabbing her cider for another sip. Moira passed her the plate of meat while she gathered up the roast vegetables and bread rolls she'd prepared earlier. 'He'll fix the inn up, sell it to the highest bidder and he'll be on his way.'

'You don't know that.'

'I've seen it before, Moira.'

Moira sighed, pausing before leading the way into the dining room. 'At least try to be civil. And whether or not he sticks around, there's no harm in enjoying the view while he is here. Who knows? He might stick around if he had a reason to.'

'It's not that simple.'

'But it could be, Brigid.'

Moira led the way into the dining room, placing the platters she held on the middle of the table and sat next to Lee who was at the head of the table. Alex sat at the other end of the table, with Aislinn sitting in the highchair between him and Moira. Brigid placed the meat on the table and took a seat at the only chair available—opposite Moira, next to Alex.

She wondered what it would take to wipe that smug look off his face.

Chapter 5

They ate in silence for a while. Well, everyone except Aislinn, who kept staring at Alex. For a moment, Brigid watched as Alex stared back at the little girl. He seemed awkward for a moment, until he tugged on one of her curly locks and 'stole' her nose. At that point, Aislinn simply smiled, blushed, and turned to her mother.

'I like him, Mammy,' she said in her sweet little voice.

She swore she could see the shade of Alex's cheeks deepen a little.

'What's your family like, Alex?' Moira asked. 'Lee and I were childhood sweethearts, so our family Christmases can get rather … interesting … but a lot of fun.'

If there was one thing about Moira, she was good at making conversation. Of course, Brigid figured Lee had got to know Alex a little while helping him with renovations, but she had a feeling that Moira's questions were more for Brigid's sake than for her and Lee. She was still sceptical about him. But Moira was right—there was no harm in enjoying the view. The tall, strong, muscular view with flashing mischievous eyes and perfect white teeth peeking out from his side grin.

'I, ahh,' Alex paused a moment, wiping his mouth with a napkin. 'I don't really … have … any family.'

Moira's eyes widened, and Lee was looking directly at Alex. But Brigid couldn't take her eyes off him. He shifted in his seat a little, and Brigid felt the edge of his shoe rest against hers. She felt a tingle through her body, like the electric shock she'd felt when she poked him the other day, though not as strong and surprising. It was more like a slow soothing pulse throughout her body.

'I don't have any siblings,' Alex continued. 'My parents didn't have any siblings either, so I guess you could say it runs in the family.' He laughed—just a little. It was a deep rumble that sent her body vibrating. His foot moved to rest gently on top of hers. 'My mother died when I was a child, so it was just my Dad and I for a long time. He lined up my apprenticeship for me and we worked together for a few years before he passed away.'

'I'm so sorry,' Moira said quietly. Brigid wasn't sure whether she looked sad or shocked.

Alex placed his hands under the table, his napkin in hand. He shrugged. 'The doctors said his heart failed him, but I think he was just missing Ma too much. I like to think he's with her, living the dream, doing everything they missed out on while they were alive.'

'That's sweet,' Moira said, a smile tugging at her lips, her eyes glistening from unshed tears.

Brigid didn't say anything, but she thought it was sweet, too. She'd always thought her mammy was waiting, somewhere out there, for her daddy to join her. She figured it must be how some people deal with grief, but she believed every part of it. She felt the warmth of what she figured must be Alex's hand rest on her knee that was peeking out from her dress. Involuntarily, she flinched, taking in a sharp breath, slamming her knees into the underside of the table. She could see the mischievous flash in his eyes again—the green a little lighter—his amusement clear.

'God, Brigid!' Moira said. 'What's wrong?'

'Sorry,' she muttered. 'I just thought I felt something brush against my leg.' She glared at Alex. 'It … freaked me out. But you don't have a cat, so I must have been imagining things.'

Alex raised an eyebrow at her, and she could feel the warmth spreading to her cheeks. God, he made her look like a fool. She shouldn't be letting him do this to her. She shouldn't be feeling things for him. But as it was, even a glance her way from him sent her stomach flipping. She wished she could slap him.

But that would be rude in front of her friends who had no idea what was going on underneath their table.

'You don't like cats?' Alex asked, his lips curving upwards at the side.

'No, I don't.'

She hadn't meant for the words to sound so icy, but she was hoping he got the hint. She couldn't be involved with him. He was exactly the kind of guy she could fall for—hard and fast—and when he left, she'd be left heartbroken. Right now, she had to focus on her and the baby in her belly.

'Lee tells me you came from Australia, Alex,' Moira said. It was more a statement than a question.

'Ahh, yes. Well, sort of,' he said. Brigid felt her forehead crease. 'I was actually living in Paris for two years before coming here, but I was born in Australia and lived there until then.'

'Why'd you leave Paris?' Brigid said, her tone still flat. God, if she'd lived in Paris, she didn't think she'd want to leave. But then, she'd never left Ireland before.

He squinted at her. 'To fix up the inn, of course.'

She didn't believe it was the sole reason. 'Did you leave someone behind?'

'What?'

'You know, a woman.' She drew out the syllables of *woman*. She knew she probably shouldn't be pushing him like this—not in front of Lee and Moira, at least, and especially not in front of Aislinn, but she was busy playing with her food. 'Surely you weren't in Paris for two years without getting close to a woman.'

His jaw clenched, and she knew she hit a nerve. So, he had left a woman behind, just like she'd thought. He was *exactly* the type of man she'd thought he was.

'Huh,' she said, trying not to smile. 'I guess it didn't work out then?'

'No, it didn't.' His eyes had deepened in colour again, shading over, and his tone was flat.

It made her shudder.

Lee cleared his throat after a moment of awkward silence. 'Alex is a painter by trade, Moira, and has worked on a lot of building projects with one of his friends, so he's doing a lot of the renovations himself.'

'I'm so glad you're renovating that poor inn,' Moira said, the disturbance forgotten. 'It's a shame it got so run-down, but it'll look good when it's finished.'

'That's what I'm aiming for,' Alex said, sipping his cider. 'It'll be good to see it thrive.'

'If it gets the chance,' Brigid muttered before she could stop herself.

Alex's eyes shot towards her and she felt like a child. She didn't like the feeling. But when she looked up at his eyes, they looked almost … hurt?

'What's that supposed to mean?' he said, his voice low, agitated.

'I—' she stammered. Why couldn't she think of something to say?

'Brigid loves that inn,' Moira said. Brigid glared at her. God, how the hell had the whole dinner conversation turned on her when she'd hardly said a thing? Granted, what she had said wasn't exactly nice. Or polite. Or respectful. 'She's worried you plan on selling it to the highest bidder and leaving once it's gone. It's happened before, Alex, with a lot of businesses in town. They were bought out and changed so they didn't keep their old charm. We don't want to see it happen to the inn, so please forgive her for being so … wary.' Moira shot a look at Brigid on the last word and she knew what she was trying to do.

But she should stop. And she certainly didn't appreciate her and Lee telling her life story and concerns to this arrogant stranger. She glanced at Alex, but he didn't look her way. He just shrugged, his face somewhat expressionless.

'I can understand why you'd all be a bit wary, but I've also read some good books with terrible covers,' he said, leaning back in his chair. 'But, if it puts your minds at ease, I don't plan on selling the inn.'

***

The whole dinner had been intense.

It was clear that Brigid was close to Moira and Lee. She seemed too comfortable at their house to just be a guest for the night. And he was certain she hadn't been happy he was there to join them for dinner. In his defence, he hadn't known she would be there. But he also wouldn't have declined coming if he knew.

He didn't know why he touched Brigid's leg, but he'd be lying if he said he didn't find her response amusing. After the delicious meal and the awkward dinner conversation, everyone seemed to relax a little. He'd complimented Moira on making the best roast he'd ever had the pleasure of eating, and he'd enjoyed watching Brigid playing with Aislinn, acting equally as sad as the child was when she was being sent to bed. She was clearly good with kids, which was probably just as well, especially if she was having a child of her own. But even though he knew the child was Darcy's, he couldn't help but see a brief vision of what she would look like playing with kids who looked a lot like her, and a lot like Alex.

Shoot.

Already she was getting into his head. He shouldn't be thinking like that. After the way she talked to him at the dinner table, he was sure he'd only be making himself look like a fool when he told her about his plan. That is, if she'd even listen to what his plan was. He let out the breath of air he hadn't realised he'd been holding onto. He didn't want to get his hopes up. But Brigid was his only chance.

She'd glared at him when she said to their hosts that she was going home, and he said he should leave too. Sure, the only reason he'd said that was because he wanted to talk to her, and since she was sort of avoiding him at work ...

He supposed if he lost his chance tonight, he could arrange a meeting with her at work tomorrow to talk business. Him being the boss, she wouldn't be able to refuse. But he didn't want to pull that card. Not with her. The inn was close enough for Alex to walk to Lee's place, and since he hadn't seen a car out front of their place when he got there, he figured Brigid must have walked from her place too.

He was relieved to find he was right.

'Brigid!' he called after her. She'd raced off before he'd finished saying his goodnights to Lee and Moira and thanking them for having him over again. He had to jog to catch up with her. 'Brigid, come on. It's dark and it's late. At least let me walk you home.'

She slowed down for him to fall into step next to her. 'You know,' she said. 'I *can* walk myself home. It's not like anything's going to happen to me. Nothing ever happens to anyone here.' She kicked a stone.

'Oh, I'm sure you could handle yourself even if something did,' he teased. 'I mean, you're a strong woman with a mind of her own. I hate to think what you would have done to Darcy if I hadn't stepped in the way for you.'

She glanced up at him, briefly, before continuing to walk. She let out a sigh. 'What do you want, Alex?'

He spread his arms out in surrender. 'I just want to talk. And make sure you get home safely. I can't have anything happening to you, after all. Especially since the inn couldn't run without you.' She stopped walking, looking up at him, her eyes curious. 'Don't think I hadn't noticed, Brigid. You do more than your job title entails.'

'Ailbe and I both had to take on more responsibilities when we couldn't afford to keep anyone else on,' she said, as if explaining the obvious.

'You know, I would believe that, if Moira didn't bring up how much you love the inn.'

She shrugged. 'You got me. What are you going to do about it, boss?'

'What makes it so special to you?' he asked.

Her eyes softened, and she stared across the street briefly before dropping her gaze to the ground. Her arms were crossed. 'I guess I just saw it as my freedom—something that wasn't copying anyone else or following in anyone's footsteps. It was entirely me. My decision to work there, not Daddy's. Do you know how it feels to do something on your own for the first time and have it work for you?' She didn't give him a chance to answer, but he was relieved she was opening up to him—even just a little. It might make his proposition a bit easier. 'And Ailbe loves it,' she continued. 'He pretty much took me in when I started working there. He's been more of a father to me than my own daddy.'

He nudged her chin gently with his hand, urging her to look at him. When her eyes connected with his, it really did take his breath away, and made him want to protect this woman any way he could. 'I meant what I said,' he said. She swallowed, her eyes searching his. 'I don't plan on selling the inn.'

'Good,' she whispered.

'But,' he said slowly. 'I may need your help to save it.'

Her brow crinkled. 'How so?'

'I only have six months to fix it up and make it successful or I'll be sent out of the country and it *will* be sold to the highest bidder.'

'I don't understand,' she said, shaking her head.

He paused, taking a deep breath. 'The attorney dropped by this afternoon. The original agreement was that I had a year to make the business successful and it would stay mine. I could stay here. But he informed me that it's been reduced to six months.'

She shook her head. 'Six months isn't enough time,' she whispered.

'But it's all we have.'

He thought he could see her eyes glistening. 'What makes you think I can help?'

'Marry me.'

There, he'd said it. And he was holding his breath for her reply. Her eyes widened, and a long moment passed before she blinked, a laugh escaping between her pretty lips. He furrowed his brow.

'Are you mad?' she said. 'I think you've had too many ciders.' She started walking again, but he grabbed hold of her arm, stopping her.

'I'm not drunk, Brigid. I'm serious.'

She searched his eyes as though she were desperately looking for something, *anything* to show her that this was all a joke. But she wouldn't find it. Because he was more serious than he'd ever been in his life.

'God,' she breathed. 'You *are* serious, aren't you?'

He nodded, but before she could answer, he spoke again. 'It would be a marriage of convenience, of course.' She raised both eyebrows, her jaw dropping slightly. 'You need help with your situation, I need help with mine.'

'My *situation*—' she started.

'Is that you're pregnant, your daddy is so strict that he'll cast you out if he finds out, and the *bastard* who did this to you is a pathetic excuse of a man who made you feel like a fool for believing anything he said.'

Her mouth dropped open even further and she snapped it shut. Her eyes had a hint of wild flashing through them, but she looked to be considering his words.

'Brigid, I can help you. You can say the child is mine, and I will raise it as my own.' He took hold of both of her hands, relieved she didn't pull away. 'I'll look after you and *our* child—our children—if we fall in love and wish to have more. You'll never have to worry about anything.'

She let out a deep shaky breath. He hoped the proposition was tempting enough for her. At least, it would get her out of trouble. 'And you?' she whispered.

'I can get citizenship and the inn is ours for keeps.'

'So, you really don't plan on leaving?'

He shook his head. 'Carrick Fitzpatrick left this inn to me for a reason. I can't just give it up. I plan to stay here for good, and you can make that possible.'

He could see her chest rising and falling with short quick breaths, and he might have been aroused had he not been nervous as hell. 'Brigid, please,' he said, squeezing her hands a little tighter. 'You're my only hope.'

For a moment, he'd seen something in her eyes, something that made his heart flip, and he was certain she was going to say yes. Then, there was a slight change in her expression, and he feared she was going to say no.

But he knew he couldn't breathe until he knew.

Chapter 6

Brigid hadn't slept. How was she supposed to when her mind was so wired? She could have passed it off for a dream had she actually been able to sleep, but as the first rays of sunlight started peeking through the slit in her curtains, she knew she'd have to face him with an answer. An answer she still wasn't sure on. All night, her mind replayed their exchange after his proposal.

'I don't even know you, Alex,' she'd said. 'We *just* met.'

He still hadn't let go of her hands, but his gentle squeezing made her feel secure—made her feel he wasn't lying about looking after her.

'What better way to get to know someone than to marry them?' The way he said it with ease and confidence made her heart do flips in her chest. 'Besides, after tonight, you officially know more about me than I know about you.'

'I still think you're holding something back.' Like the whole leaving a woman in Paris thing. And why had he moved to Paris in the first place? Had he left a woman there, too?

His eyes shadowed again, like they had when she'd mentioned it at the dinner table. 'It's nothing of consequence,' he said. But she wasn't convinced.

She'd asked him for time to sort her thoughts. He'd said time was something they didn't have much of, but she could take as long as she needed. But he made a point—she still had no idea how she would hide the whole being pregnant thing from her daddy, or what she would do when he found out. She wasn't one to just jump into marriage, but his offer was tempting. After all, it *was* a marriage of convenience. She hadn't known of anyone having a marriage of convenience in the twenty-first century—no one she knew, anyway. No doubt, they still existed, they just weren't as common. And something was common with marriages of convenience—there were conditions attached.

She obviously had more to benefit from this … arrangement … than he had, but he'd had her convinced when he said he didn't want to leave and that he cared about the inn. But it was insane. It was absolutely, ridiculously ludicrous. And it made perfect sense. It wasn't the worst idea ever. He *was* handsome, extremely easy on the eyes. They obviously had some kind of chemistry to keep things interesting. And he *seemed* genuine …

She groaned, rolling out of bed. She wasn't going to be able to get any sleep, so she may as well get dressed and head to work. There was no point in delaying the inevitable. She would have to give an answer to Alex today. Like he said, they were short on time and every moment longer she took to answer him was a moment less they had to work out how to save the inn. She pulled her clothes on—jeans, a white shirt, her grey jacket, and her boots—and headed to the kitchen.

'Coffee?' Colleen asked as soon as she got to the doorway.

'Do you have to ask?'

Colleen's eyes went wide when she looked at her. 'Did you get any sleep last night?' Brigid shook her head. 'Didn't you go to Lee and Moira's for dinner?'

She nodded. She'd never been able to not sleep well after roast night, and Colleen knew that. Brigid scanned the room. 'Where's Daddy?'

'Out on his paper run.'

Brigid slid into her seat at the table, accepting the coffee Colleen handed to her. 'Alex was there.'

'Your new boss?' Colleen joined her at the table.

She cringed. She didn't like to think of him as her boss—he'd said himself the place couldn't run without her—especially, if she was going to agree to marry him, which she still wasn't sure about. Colleen would tell her she was mad for even considering it, and she'd be right.

'Well, he kind of … proposed.' Colleen's eyes went wide. 'A marriage of convenience, of course,' she added, before her sister could say anything. She lowered her voice. 'You know, with my … situation.' She hated using the word, but she didn't want to haphazardly say she was pregnant because, knowing her luck, that's when her daddy would walk in. 'And he could get citizenship so he can keep the inn, otherwise he'll have to leave in six months and the inn will be sold.'

Colleen took a sip of coffee, staring at Brigid, not blinking. Slowly, she placed the cup back on the table. 'That's so—'

'Insane?'

'*Romantic*!' She drew out the syllables. Brigid was sure she could see hearts in Colleen's eyes. She sighed, Colleen was supposed to try to talk her out of it, not be all lovey-dovey over it.

'Don't you think it's a little bit insane, at least?'

Colleen shrugged. 'It makes sense.'

'What?'

'Think about it Brigid,' Colleen leaned closer to her. 'You don't have another plan, and you don't have much time. I've seen him going into the hardware store with Lee—he's hot as hell. And it saves the inn. There's no way you can lose.'

She sat silently for a moment, letting what Colleen said sink it. Then, she sighed. 'God, I hate it when you're right.'

She savoured the coffee rolling through her mouth and wondered if she should even be drinking it. Wasn't coffee one of those things you should give up if your pregnant? She turned the cup between her hands. It wasn't *definite*, yet. Surely, one cup wouldn't hurt. She was glad their sensitive conversation was over, because right at that moment, their daddy walked in, his paper in his hand.

'Good morning, girls,' he said, grabbing a cup, and filling it with the coffee Colleen prepared. 'What's the plan today?'

'Work,' Brigid and Colleen said in unison. Their daddy scratched his chin, studying Brigid. Colleen worked as a nurse at the local hospital—he was proud of her, working a job where she literally helped save lives. But he'd never approved of Brigid working at a rundown inn, even though she practically managed it.

'Hmm,' Daddy said. 'I ran into Darcy on my paper run, Brigid.' He took a seat at the table with his coffee and his paper. He started flicking through the pages. 'He said you had something to tell me.'

Brigid felt her heart skip a beat, her breath stopping, and shot a look towards Colleen whose eyes were wide. She could feel her blood boiling. How *dare* he talk to her daddy! He wanted her to be cast out of her family, especially if she refused to get rid of the baby. If she could just …

'They're not together anymore,' Colleen blurted, sending a reassuring wink towards Brigid.

Well, at least she thought it was supposed to be reassuring. At this stage, she was trying not to freak out about what her sister was trying to do, and how much she was going to say.

'What do you mean?' He directed the question at Brigid.

'Well, I ... he ... he, umm ...' God, how much information could *she* give out?

'They broke up, Daddy,' Colleen said. Thank God she didn't say why.

He didn't take his eyes off Brigid. 'Is this true, Brigid?'

Slowly, she nodded. 'It didn't work out, but it's no big deal.'

He reached out and placed his hand on hers. 'I'll make it right. Darcy is making a big mistake. I'll talk to his daddy, he can talk some sense into him, and this can all be forgo—'

'No!' Brigid barely heard the word come from her mouth. His eyes widened.

'No?'

'I—' God, now what? 'I don't want to be with him, Daddy.'

'Why not? He's a good match.' His voice was stern, and she was starting to feel it all unravelling.

Colleen sighed and when she spoke, she sounded bored. 'Because he's an ass, Daddy, and she's found another man.'

'Language, child.'

Colleen scoffed. 'I'm twenty-three, Daddy. And Brigid is twenty-five. She can deal with her man problems herself.'

He glared at Colleen, but his gaze softened a little

when he looked back at Brigid. 'How serious are you and your *new man*?'

'They're engaged,' Colleen said. 'She was just about to tell you, *right Brigid*?'

Her daddy raised an eyebrow. 'Ahh, yes, I was,' she said hesitantly. She guessed there was no backing out of it now. 'He proposed last night, and I said yes.'

He glanced down at her left hand. 'No ring?'

Shoot. 'He, ahh, it didn't … fit. So, he's getting it resized.' She'd have to remember to buy a ring. She shouldn't expect him to get one for her for a marriage of convenience, should she?

'What's his name?'

'Alex Carter.' She savoured his name as it rolled over her tongue. She'd have to change her name from Brigid Murphy, she supposed. *Mrs Brigid Carter*—it did have a nice ring to it.

He pulled his hand back. 'The new inn owner.' It wasn't a question. She should have known he would put the pieces together. She hadn't wanted to lie to his face, but she felt she was going to have to. 'I heard he only arrived on Sunday gone.'

'He visited a few months back,' she lied. She glanced over at Colleen. Her eyes were wide, worried. She knew she'd be in trouble if her daddy discovered she was lying. 'To see what needed to be done to the inn, and he left to organise his move.' Colleen was shaking her head slowly, but she couldn't change her story now. 'We kept in touch. He wanted to be updated on everything that was happening at the inn and in the town. I guess it was just the start of something.'

He didn't blink, and he stayed silent for a moment, making Brigid very uncomfortable with her story. Finally, he sipped his coffee and continued flicking through the pages of his newspaper. She let out the breath she was holding onto.

'Alex will come to dinner on Friday night,' he said. 'I need to make sure he's suitable for my oldest daughter. You and Colleen will cook. He will dress formally, understand?'

She nodded her head. How was she going to ask Alex to do all this? It wasn't exactly part of the arrangement.

'Well?'

'Yes, Daddy.'

***

Alex felt agitated, nervous, and a little infuriated. Of course, he had expected she might not give an answer straight away, but he hadn't expected that he wouldn't be able to sleep until he knew. He sipped his coffee that he held in one hand and continued slapping some paint on the weatherboard with his other hand. He didn't know what he would do if Brigid said no. He'd hate to see this inn go, especially since he'd put so much work into it.

He'd meant every word he said to her. He would look after the child as his own. She'd never have to worry about anything. He'd treat her right. And he knew they would be able to fall in love. Already, they had an attraction that couldn't be ignored. He'd never wanted to have a woman as much as he wanted Brigid. No woman has affected him as much as she has.

So, when he saw her walking towards him like a woman on a mission, her brow furrowed and a frown on her face, it would suffice to say that his nerves were getting the better of him.

'I take it you've come to a decision?' he said hesitantly, putting his paint brush and coffee down. She stopped in front of him.

'Where would we live?' Her eyes were interrogating, her voice frantic.

'Here, of course. I've got a room—'

'I want my own room,' she said. 'You haven't bought me, I will not sleep with you.'

'Yet,' he teased. Her eyes widened. 'Relax, Brigid. I'm not going to force you into anything.'

He felt the sting of her hand across his cheek, making his jaw start throbbing again. It had only just stopped aching from Darcy's punch.

'What the *hell* was that for?'

'For making me look like a fool at dinner last night.'

He made her look like a fool? She'd practically tried to trip him up and interrogate him! If anyone looked like a fool, it was him. And he still proposed to her afterwards.

'I keep my job, and you'll keep paying my wage,' she continued. He rubbed his eyes. Was she going to be this demanding throughout their marriage? 'I know you said you'll look after me—us—but I am an independent woman. I don't need charity.'

'How about a pay rise?'

'What?'

He shrugged. 'Comes with the promotion.' Whatever her answer was going to be, he'd intended on actually giving her the title that she already worked and paying her fairly. To be honest, he hadn't thought she might have stopped working. God, the inn would truly be screwed if she stopped working.

'Promotion?' she repeated, hesitantly.

He placed his hands on her shoulders, allowing them to move down her arms to hold her hands. Her high-strung expression softened. 'Well you've been doing all the work of a manager around here,' he said. 'It's only fair that you get the actual title and the corrected pay that comes with it.'

'Are … are you serious?' Her eyes searched his and he felt warmth spreading through his body. And he knew he would probably meet any demand this beautiful woman made because he was already falling for her.

'It's yours,' he said, his voice low, soothing.

She dropped her gaze. 'I guess that makes me look bad for slapping you.'

He scrunched his nose momentarily. 'Only a little,' he teased.

'Sorry about that,' she said, fluttering her eyes back up to connect with his.

He felt his heart skip a beat and something

stirring below his belt. God, did she know how gorgeous she was? When she let him, he would show her exactly how gorgeous she was. He'd leave no part of her uncherished. He planned to make sure she felt his appreciation over every inch of her body. But he would wait for her to come to him. Like he said, he wouldn't push her. But he wouldn't mind pushing her up against this wall and having his way with her …

'How's your jaw?'

She reached her hand up to touch where Darcy's fist connected with him. He groaned, a combination of the pain throbbing through his face and her touch stirring something inside him—something deep and uncontrollable that would make it freaking hard to wait for her to come to him.

'It was feeling fine until you slapped me.' She grimaced a little, her eyes apologetic. 'But I'll forgive you—this time.'

She smiled, a true genuine smile. The one he'd been waiting to see since the second he first saw her. It looked good on her. The way her teeth peeked out from behind her luscious pink lips that he wanted to taste. The way her eyes lit up and accentuated her auburn hair that he wanted to run his hands through. The way her chin lifted slightly, drawing his attention to the suppleness of her neck he wanted to kiss …

'So, umm …' she started, snapping him out of his thoughts.

'Do you have any more requests, my dear?'

'Just one.' She hesitated.

He raised his eyebrow, curious, but at the same time feeling like he didn't want to know what it was. 'What is it?'

'You have to prove to my daddy that you're right for me.'

She said the words quickly, and it took a moment for his mind to catch up with them. '*What*?'

She grimaced. 'He wants to meet you and see if you're right for me, and you need to convince him you are.'

'*I* have to convince him?' He could feel his body shaking. He let go of her hands and ran his fingers through his hair. *Shoot*. That wasn't part of the plan. 'How does that fit into a *marriage of convenience?*'

'Well, if he's not convinced, then this won't happen,' she said, pointing at him then at herself. 'If he is convinced, you'll get your citizenship and I'll be saving face with my daddy.'

He let out an exasperated sigh. He hadn't factored in that he might have to try to win over a strict father ground in tradition. It mightn't be so hard if Brigid's sister were married already, but she wasn't. He would be setting the standard. And Brigid's daddy would be bringing out all the hooks and turns to make sure he was perfect for his daughter.

'*Fine*,' he said.

'Thank you,' Brigid whispered. 'Tomorrow night for dinner, six o'clock. Don't be late and—' her eyes were pleading. 'Wear a suit.'

'A *suit*?' What was he getting himself into?

She nodded. 'Dinners at our place with guests are formal occasions. We'll all be dressed up. It's kind of … his thing. Oh, and if he asks you how we met, you visited the inn when you were first informed about it, so two months ago, and we met there. We've kept in touch since, talking business and … us.'

'You want me to lie to him.' His head was reeling.

'Well, I can't tell him I've only known you for five days, can I?'

He sighed, bending down to sweep a kiss onto her cheek. Even *that* required a lot of effort to not push it to something more. God, if he was going through all of this, impressing her father just for a marriage of convenience, he was going to want something in return. Eventually. He wasn't one to go back on his word. But he hoped she wouldn't take her time.

Impressing fathers to be with a woman wasn't what he did. Betty's father never battered an eyelid at him. He just handed him a beer and went on his way. Rob Henders, Liz's dad, was already like family when they were involved. Not to mention that he didn't know about their involvement. If he did, he probably wouldn't be allowed to come to any more Henders' Christmases.

'Dinner tomorrow, then,' he said. She smiled at him again, and he hoped he'd be able to see more of that smile. She opened her mouth to speak, but he continued, knowing what she'd be thinking. 'I'll wear a suit, be on my best behaviour, be consistent with your story, and … impress … your daddy. Is there anything I should bring?'

She sighed. 'Bring some Irish Whiskey, single malt. You can get a bottle from *The Hound & The Harp*, Lee knows which one. It's his favourite, so at least you'll be off to a good start.'

'Tomorrow, then,' he said, watching her walk towards the new front door of the inn.

She smiled at him, draping her hand along the adornments on the door. 'I like this.'

Then she went inside and, when he was sure she couldn't hear, he cursed, throwing his hat onto the ground. Asking Brigid to marry him made him nervous as hell. Trying to impress her daddy was going to be a near-on impossible task. But it would all be worth it.

At least, he hoped it would.

Chapter 7

Alex took the steps up to Brigid's front door with a bounce in his step. He'd been nervous about this dinner up until the first rays of sunshine were shining on his face. That was another thing he had to organise for the rooms—new curtains that weren't in tatters, and maybe rearranging the furniture so the beds faced the other way. Maybe Brigid could help him with the decorating and rearranging. He'd hit the floor running to start his day, taking a trip to Cork to get a license to marry—it had been a tricky task, convincing the celebrant to grant him the license, being so soon after his arrival in Ireland, his conditions with the inn, and wanting to be married so quickly.

'It sounds a lot like you're just trying to gain

citizenship, Mr Carter,' the celebrant had said, eyeing him suspiciously.

'She's pregnant,' he'd replied. 'I'm just trying to do right by her.'

Apparently, pregnancy was grounds enough to grant a license without giving the usual period of notice. While he was up there, he'd thought he may as well do some shopping. Although Cork was only about half an hour away from Kinsale, he didn't anticipate that he'd be able to make trips there very often. Besides, there were some things he had to order to pick up in a week's time.

He took a deep breath and knocked on the door, holding a bottle of single malt Irish Whiskey that Lee assured him was Mr Murphy's favourite, and an elaborate bouquet of flowers in his other hand. Brigid answered the door, looking somewhat flustered. She seemed to relax a little to see it was him, especially when her eyes dropped to the bottle of whiskey.

'It's almost six,' she whispered.

'Hey, I'm not late.' He handed the bouquet out to her. 'These are for you. You look beautiful.' Beautiful was a bit of an understatement, really. She was the look of pure perfection in her knee-length deep purple dress. It was more on the modest side, but it hugged her body in all the right places, still managing to make him want to rip the dress off her to reveal the beauty that lay beneath it.

He saw a blush creep across her already flustered face. 'Thank you,' she said. She moved aside for him to come in.

'Are you okay?' he asked, noticing she was holding the stem of the bouquet so tightly that her knuckles had paled.

'I just hope tonight goes well,' she said.

He leaned down, planting a kiss on her cheek. 'It will.'

He hadn't thought she might be more nervous about the dinner than he would be. He supposed she had a lot more to lose than he did if it didn't go well. He'd get sent out of the country and lose the inn, but she could actually lose everything. He wondered if she would still consider eloping with him if her daddy disapproved. And would he be willing to go up against her daddy if that were the case?

She reached for his hand and weaved her fingers between his. He looked down at their hands, marvelling at how perfectly they fit together, wondering how on earth it could just feel so ... right. He understood why she was holding his hand—they had to convince her daddy they were in love, that he was right for her, and to do that, they needed to be somewhat affectionate with each other. But he'd be lying if he said it didn't feel right. He brought his gaze to meet hers.

The blush in her cheeks deepened. 'Just to ... umm ... help our case,' she muttered.

She led him towards the dining room, her hand gripping his tighter the closer they got. He was surprised to see how elaborately the table was set in the dining room. The food was already spread on the table—some kind of baked chicken with bacon and mushrooms, bread rolls and a salad—and her daddy and sister were already seated.

'Daddy, Colleen, this is Alex,' Brigid said.

Her daddy was the first to rise from his seat, extending his hand out to Alex. 'Pleasure to meet you, Mr Murphy,' Alex said, gripping his hand. 'I brought this for you.' He handed the bottle towards him. 'I heard you're a whiskey fan.'

He seemed to consider Alex for a moment before a grin spread across his face. He took the bottle from Alex and placed it on the buffet table along the wall with a number of other decanters and glasses. 'You're a good lad,' he said. He was dressed in a suit which looked as though it had been recently tailored for him.

'Nice to meet you, Alex,' Colleen said. She was just as dressed up as Brigid.

'And you, too.'

'Please, sit.' He indicated to the seat next to him, then towards the food. 'The girls have been busy, as you can see.'

He took his seat, feeling a little uncomfortable that he would be sitting right next to Brigid's daddy, but he figured that was the whole reason he was here, right? To impress her daddy. It only made sense that he would be the topic of conversation. Out of the corner of his eye, he saw Colleen take the flowers from Brigid, whispering something into her ear. Brigid blushed, before smoothing her dress and sitting next to Alex.

'It's good to see you own a suit, Alex,' Mr Murphy said, eyeing him off. 'Every businessman needs a good suit.'

Admittedly, it was by no means tailored. Alex just had the right sort of body to fill out a normal suit nicely. It wasn't exactly cheap, but it also wasn't an Italian suit or anything flash. He hesitated a moment.

'I'm actually not a businessman,' he said. Mr Murphy raised an eyebrow. 'I'm a painter by trade.'

Mr Murphy rubbed his chin. 'Is that very profitable?'

'I've never been short on work,' he said confidently. 'There's always someone who needs something painted. And it's come in very handy with the inn.'

'Alex has just finished painting the outside of the inn, Daddy,' Brigid said, her voice sweet and quiet. Alex couldn't help but think it didn't suit her. He was so used to the abrupt way she spoke to him. 'It's looking really good.'

'I'm not sure that inn could ever look good,' he said gruffly.

Alex felt his eyes widening. Brigid dropped her gaze to her lap where her hands fiddled with a thread on her dress. How could he think that? He cleared his throat. 'Actually, Mr Murphy, the old inn has a lot of charm to it. By the time it's finished it'll look the best it ever has.'

Mr Murphy's mouth dropped open and he looked as though he were about to say something when Colleen came back into the room, placing the vase of flowers that Alex brought on the buffet table.

'Daddy, you're not starting the interrogations already, are you?' she said. 'The food is getting cold.'

She started dishing up some food onto her daddy's plate and then her own, while Brigid carefully placed some of the chicken on Alex's plate before putting some on her own. He smiled at Brigid, catching her eye.

'It smells amazing,' he said. 'You did a wonderful job, dear.'

'Actually, Colleen cooked,' she said, picking up the bowl of salad. 'I made the salad.'

He crinkled his nose. 'I'm not a big salad fan.'

He was sure he saw her lip twitch; her eyes were flashing. She placed the bowl next to his plate and got a large scoop of salad out, placing it on his plate next to the chicken. He didn't shift his eyes from her.

'Well,' she said. 'You had better learn to be, *dear*.'

'Yes, ma'am,' he teased.

She looked as though she was struggling not to laugh, or smile, by the time she'd finished putting the salad on her own plate. He breathed a sigh of relief. He actually preferred salad over vegetables, but he couldn't think of anything else to try to get her to relax. Besides, it was all part of his plan to impress her daddy. Somehow.

As soon as Mr Murphy took a bite of his meal, the interrogation started again. Alex was starting to think he might be harder to impress than he'd first thought. But then, it wasn't exactly something he'd planned on having to do when he asked Brigid to marry him.

'So, if you're not a businessman, what do you plan to do with the inn?'

'Well, I plan to keep it, if I can,' he said. 'I just have to work out how to make it successful. I'm sure Brigid can help me in that aspect.' He glanced over at Brigid, who was staring at him, her eyes softened. She flicked her eyes back down towards the plate.

'Do you have your citizenship sorted, Alex?'

He hesitated. He knew it would only be a matter of time before this topic would come up, but he hadn't expected Mr Murphy would be out for blood. 'I have a plan in place,' he said.

'So, you don't have it yet?' He had a smug look on his face. Honestly, he'd much rather be wiping that look off his face than bending over backwards to impress him.

'No.'

'Well, you would need it to keep the inn,' Mr Murphy pointed out.

'I am aware of that.' Alex could tell his tone was flat. He could also see Colleen's eyes shooting between him and their daddy. He felt Brigid tense next to him.

***

She wanted to crawl under the table, curl into a ball and stay there until this was all over. Colleen had assured her she would help keep Daddy under control. She'd thought they could pull this off—they all did. But Daddy wasn't holding anything back and he was clearly convinced of one thing: there was only one man good enough for Brigid, and that man wasn't Alex.

'I'm well aware that getting married would make it significantly easier to gain citizenship,' her daddy said. 'Well, it would guarantee it, actually. Is that why you want to marry my daughter?'

Brigid lost control over her fork at possibly the worst time. It made a loud clattering noise as it bounced off her plate, off the table and onto the floor. She felt her cheeks flush. In fact, all of her felt flushed. This was all going wrong, so terribly wrong.

'Daddy, can we please enjoy the meal?' Colleen said, sweetly, but sternly.

God, she didn't feel like she'd ever be able to talk to her daddy like that. Colleen had always been the favourite—that's probably why she could get away with it. But Brigid? She had to be perfect. She felt as though she was on the verge of hyperventilating, or crying, or something, when she felt Alex's hand take hold of hers under the table, squeezing it gently.

Alex sighed. 'You know, you're right,' he said. *What was he saying?* 'Marrying would just about guarantee me citizenship.'

The look on her daddy's face was hardening, but he was smiling, as though he knew he'd found Alex out. For a moment, she was convinced he had.

'But,' Alex continued, ignoring the look. 'That's not why I want to marry Brigid. In the end, the inn is just an inn, and like you pointed out, I'm a painter, not a businessman. Anyone could really take over the inn—I don't have to. It's a material thing. But this—' he held up her hand, still squeezing it gently, but firmly, reassuringly. 'This isn't. *This* is real. I have never met a woman like Brigid before. No one has ever caught my attention in the way she has. She's beautiful, smart, and perfection at its finest. She knows how to challenge me and make me want to better myself. I knew I wanted to make her my wife the moment I laid eyes on her. Getting to know her only confirmed it. So, if I was marrying for citizenship, it's not for the inn. It's for Brigid.'

Brigid's heart skipped a beat. She knew he was just saying these things to make her daddy like him. But *damn*. He was a good actor. He'd had her believing he really meant what he said—every word. And she wished he really did mean it. But she couldn't let herself be fooled. He'd proposed a marriage of convenience. Not a real marriage. Not love. Convenience.

Even though he'd had her fooled, and going by the look on Colleen's face, she thought it was the most romantic thing she'd ever heard, her daddy didn't batter an eyelid. Instead, he picked up his fork and started eating some more of his food. Hesitantly, they all did. A few mouthfuls in, her daddy spoke again.

'You know, Brigid was only recently seeing another man.' *No* ... 'He's a very nice man, very suitable. They were going very well until you came along. Are you the reason why they broke up?'

Alex let out a laugh and tried to regain his composure. Brigid felt her hairs standing on edge. 'Who, that bas—' he caught Brigid's widened eyes— meant to send a warning—and the slightest shake of her head. He cleared his throat. 'Ahh, yes, I did know about Darcy. And I hope I wasn't the sole reason, but I had made my intentions clear to Brigid. I think she made the right decision, anyway. I feel I had more to offer her than he did.'

Brigid knew he shouldn't have said that last bit, but how was he to know about Darcy's standing in the town? They hadn't had a chance to run through their entire non-existent story, so he was doing quite well to fill in the gaps himself. She saw her daddy's eyebrow shoot up and she held her breath. She looked over at Colleen for some help—maybe she could run an interference—but she looked just as stunned as Brigid felt. Then, her daddy laughed, a big full-bellied laugh, and Alex looked confused.

'Darcy is very well to do,' her daddy said. 'His daddy is heavily involved in the fish market and very influential in this town. Darcy's future is very promising. So, please, humour me. *What* can *you* offer her that he can't? A run-down inn? A life spent trying to make ends meet?'

Brigid kept her gaze on Alex. She shouldn't have done this to him. She shouldn't have been so worried about saving face with her daddy. She mightn't have been, had she known he was going to be so ridiculing of him. She felt ashamed, and she could feel the respect she had for her daddy dwindling. She could see the pulsing of the vein on Alex's neck, the tension of his jaw—of his whole body. God, what would she do if he decided he didn't want to go through with the marriage of convenience? She was worried Alex was going to just stand up and leave, but he stayed seated, his body firm, strong, unwavering. And when he spoke, his voice was steady, confident, and authoritative.

'Security,' he said. 'Respect. Love. A life without worrying about unnecessary things, and where she can continue doing what she loves, not succumbing to the demands of an arrogant husband. She'd be treated better than a princess. She would come with me when I travel, instead of being left behind worrying about whether or not her husband would be faithful. Because, unlike Darcy, *I* would always be faithful to Brigid.'

She'd also forgotten to mention that her daddy didn't know Darcy had been unfaithful. But when what Alex said made her daddy's mouth drop in surprise, and his eyes moved from Alex to Brigid, softening as they did, she was starting to feel he couldn't have said it any better. Her daddy hummed, taking a long drink from his glass before placing it back onto the table and examining the pattern on it. The room was dead quiet for a moment as her, Colleen, and Alex kept their eyes on her daddy. Then, he let out a slow deep breath and brought his focus back to Alex.

'When do you plan on marrying?'

Alex smiled, relaxing a little. 'As soon as we can.'

Brigid sighed a breath of relief, taking the opportunity to encourage her body to find its appetite again, and Colleen took the chance to direct the conversation onto friendlier territory.

'So, you like to travel, Alex?' she said.

Alex told them about all the places he'd been to and what he'd done at each place, and Brigid couldn't take her eyes off him, taking in all of his adventures and everywhere he still wished to see— with Brigid. He was holding her hand under the table again, and she couldn't help but feel that this whole thing was the realest thing she'd ever had. The feelings she was starting to feel for him were dangerous. He'd put on an act for her daddy, and now, she didn't know what was true and what wasn't. But if he was being honest about everything he said, maybe their marriage of convenience wouldn't be so bad after all.

Chapter 8

Brigid walked Alex out to his car after dinner. They walked in silence, feeling heavy from the intensity of their dinner. Or, at least, she was. He reached into his car, putting the key into the ignition, and turning it on, but he didn't climb in yet. Instead, he leaned against the side of the car to face her and pulled her close for a hug. She didn't resist. She rested her head against his chest, wrapping her arms around his waist, his arms around her shoulders, his hands resting against the small of her back. They stood in silence, locked in their embrace for what felt like a few minutes, but Brigid had no idea how long it was.

She closed her eyes, focussing on the steady thumping of his heart beating against his chest. He felt warm, secure, inviting. And every second longer she was in his arms gave her a little bit more courage to go back inside and face her daddy without him by her side. Her daddy hadn't held anything back in confronting Alex. There was no light conversation or getting to know him before delving straight into the heavy stuff.

But she knew it wouldn't be the end of it, even if her daddy had seemed to almost be all right with it by the end of the interrogation. She knew she would have to face him alone. Colleen wouldn't be able to pull much weight, not with this. Her daddy didn't know Darcy hadn't been faithful to her. She would be expected to explain it to him. And whether or not he would give her and Alex the go-ahead, she wouldn't know. And she didn't know about her true feelings for Alex or how he really felt about her. But she was starting to wonder if she was already in deeper than he was. And it was all because of him.

If he hadn't said all those things to her daddy so convincingly that *she* was convinced, maybe her guard would still be up. But now, her inner self was trying to rebuild that guard while a big wrecking ball kept knocking it down. She breathed in his scent— spicy with a hint of cinnamon and chocolate mixed with something uniquely him—and committed it to memory. She felt his lips press against the top of her head long enough for her to feel the rise of his chest as he breathed in her scent. It was the most intimate she'd felt with anyone in her life. She'd done much more with Darcy, but she'd never felt intimate, never felt the connection.

Alex broke the silence, but he didn't let her go. 'So, that went well.' Brigid smiled at the hint of sarcasm in his voice. 'How do you think it went?'

'Mmm …' She hummed against his chest. 'I don't want to think about it.'

'That good, huh?'

She shook her head slowly, still keeping her face buried into his chest. 'My daddy's a jackass.'

'Well, I wasn't going to say that, but …'

'But he is,' she said. 'He shouldn't have interrogated you like that. It's like he already had this formed opinion of you and he didn't want to budge. He was just … just …'

'Out for blood?' Alex offered, moving one of his hands from the small of her back to rest against the back of her head. She could feel his fingers tangling through her hair.

She pulled her head back to look up at him. 'Yes, exactly! He was out for blood. And he's a jackass for being like that.'

He moved his hand to brush her hair away from her eyes, his fingers lingering to caress her cheek. 'He just wants the best for you.'

'He doesn't know what's best for me,' she muttered, burying her face in his chest again. 'I've never been able to get his approval for anything. He's disappointed I'm not more like Colleen.'

He pulled her back, nudging her chin up to look at him. She did, reluctantly. 'Hey,' he said. 'Don't think that. If he was disappointed in you, he wouldn't have been so hard on me. I don't like how you're different around him than you are around me—it's like you were stepping on eggshells. It might be hard to see, but he *does* want what's best for you, Brigid. He just has a strange way of showing it.'

The tenderness in his eyes as they searched hers was reassuring, and it made her heart feel that everything he'd said was true, even though her mind told her it couldn't be. But there was one way to find out ...

'Did you mean what you said?' she asked tentatively. His brow furrowed slightly, as though he was confused. 'To my daddy. About us. About ... me.'

He didn't reply straight away, but his eyes kept searching hers. And when he spoke, she hadn't expected his answer. 'Every word.'

'But we're not in ... love.'

He shrugged, a smile tugging at his lips. 'Doesn't mean I don't think we will.'

She hadn't expected his answer to make her heart stop beating for a moment, or her body stop breathing, but it did. She hadn't anticipated the warmth spreading to her core, making her want him—all of him—and everything he had to offer, but it did.

'I'm going to kiss you now,' he whispered, pressing his palms gently against the small of her back.

'Wh—'

She was cut off by his lips pressing tenderly against hers and everything stopped. The wind, the traffic around them, the noise of the crickets.

Everything except for her heart, which started going into overdrive, beating at a thousand beats a minute. The chaos in her mind over how the night went was smoothing out, and all she could think about was him. Purely him—his scent, his touch, his lips on hers, his body pressing gently against hers, fuelling her desire.

And then, he pulled away. She let out a moan of disappointment, surprising herself for feeling so … needy. He smiled, touching his hand to her cheek for a brief moment.

'Goodnight, Brigid.'

'Goodnight,' she whispered.

He released her, and she took a step back, watching as he climbed into his car and drove towards the inn. For that brief moment, in his arms, his lips on hers, she'd felt like she was floating. She'd felt like she could take on anything. Letting out the breath she'd been holding on to, she turned to go back inside. And when she saw her daddy staring out the window and realised he would have seen the whole thing, she came crashing back down to earth.

It was all for show.

And *damn*, he was a good actor.

She tried to lift the boulder that just crushed her heart, building up the courage to face her daddy. Even if the kiss was for show, surely, he felt what she felt? There was no way the fire that started from one innocent kiss like that could only be felt by her. He *had* to feel it, too. And even if that part was for show, her daddy wouldn't have been able to hear what they were talking about. He couldn't have just been saying he meant it, could he? It made sense that if they *did* get married, they might fall in love one day. Heck, Brigid was already halfway there. And not knowing exactly where he stood in that scared the hell out of her.

She took a deep breath to calm herself and opened the door, her daddy already waiting for her.

***

Alex lay on his bed, staring at the patterns on the ceiling. He'd taken his jacket off but hadn't bothered to change. He didn't even try to sleep. He just had to think. He could feel the weight on his chest. He'd pulled out everything he could think of to say to Brigid's daddy to get his approval. He'd exaggerated, made things up, said all the right things. And somewhere along the line, he'd started believing it himself. And then with Brigid as he was leaving— he'd never felt so real, so … alive.

They'd both gone into the dinner knowing they would do whatever it took to get her daddy's approval. That meant looking the part. They had to look like they were in love. And when Alex saw Mr Murphy watching them from the window, he knew what he was waiting for. So, he pulled her in for an intimate hug, hoping he would give them some privacy. But he watched on, waiting for anything to make their story unbelievable. Alex hadn't wanted their first kiss to be under the scrutinizing gaze of her father. He'd wanted them to be alone—no one watching, no one giving a damn. He'd wanted to be able to kiss her with everything he had. He didn't want to hold anything back with her. He'd wanted to truly mean everything he said.

But even though the kiss wasn't what he'd wanted, it lit a fire between them. He'd felt it, and she had to have felt it, too. It was a kiss to stop all time. A kiss he didn't want to end. But he'd had to, before it got more intense in front of speculating eyes. And when it ended, he had to use all of his strength to not pull her and her beautiful vanilla-scented hair into the car with him and drive her to the courthouse, waking the celebrant and demanding he marry them now. If they were already married, they wouldn't have to deal with impressing her daddy, would they? He supposed it was better this way. Or at least, it was what Brigid wanted.

The kiss might have been for show, but what he felt was real.

And he couldn't deny it.

Brigid had asked if he meant what he'd said to her daddy. She wouldn't have asked it if she didn't believe it. He *had* meant every word—for the most part. What he said about Brigid was true. What he could offer her was true. But Mr Murphy was onto him—he needed his citizenship to keep the inn and he wasn't ready to let it go. He was nothing but an opportunist who'd found someone willing enough to help him. But it wasn't just him, and it wasn't just for the inn. Brigid needed help. *She* needed an arrangement. She didn't have to accept his proposal, but she did, because she needed this as much as he did.

But it was steadily changing from a marriage of convenience to something more.

There were emotions involved. There were lies. There were feelings. Feelings that were probably prompted by the fantasy of their whole situation. And feelings that, if he wasn't careful, could change everything.

***

'Is it true?'

Brigid sighed. 'You'll have to be more specific.'

Her daddy walked towards her, placing his hands on her shoulders. 'Was Darcy seeing someone else?'

She nodded. At least he wasn't asking about everything Alex said, because, to be honest, she couldn't say if it was true or not. She wanted to believe it—she *had* believed it—but when she realised the kiss was for show, she started thinking the hug was for show, too—that all of it was for show. And, if her daddy asked her, she wasn't sure she'd be able to lie to his face again. Not when her mind was all over the place.

He sighed, letting out a deep, slow breath. 'How serious?'

'They're engaged,' she said, her voice quiet. She was starting to feel like she'd hit a wall. She was exhausted, confused, and talking about Darcy wasn't what she wanted to do. 'I think ... I think he was seeing her the whole time we were together.'

Her daddy pulled her close to him, wrapping his arms around her—something he hadn't done for a long time. 'I'm sorry, Brigid,' he said, his voice shaking. 'I thought—'

'It's okay, Daddy,' she said, trying to stop her eyes from tearing from the sudden affection her daddy was showing.

'I just want what's best for you. It's hard without your mammy here.'

At the mention of her mammy, one of the threatening tears spilled, followed by another. She brushed the tears away with the back of her hand.

'Maybe we could try letting me make some decisions of my own, what do you think?' she said, looking up at her daddy. 'I mean, I *am* twenty-five, after all.'

He smiled, wiping away his own tears. 'Maybe I've been too hard on you.'

She crinkled her nose. 'Only a little.'

'Are you happy with Alex? Is this marriage what you want?'

She nodded. 'It is, Daddy,' she said.

She felt as though she was trying to convince herself as much as she was trying to convince him. The marriage wasn't just what she wanted. It was what she *needed*. She *needed* security. She *needed* her child to grow up with two parents, feeling loved. And Alex could offer that to her.

He took a deep, concentrated breath. 'Well, if

that's what you want,' he said. 'I'm still not convinced Alex is right for you, but it seems I'm not the best judge of character anyway. He'd better treat you right.'

'He will,' she said.

Of that, she was sure.

Chapter 9

Brigid grimaced as the sunlight hit her face when she stepped outside of her house. She felt groggy, and her stomach churned. She wasn't hungover—she knew not to drink while she was pregnant. Her head throbbed from the tear-filled night she'd just had. As soon as she'd closed the door to her bedroom and slid down to the floor, she'd felt it—alone. She may have Colleen and her daddy now, but when he found out the baby was Darcy's, and what her and Alex had was all put on, he'd be out of her life, taking Colleen with him. She would have no one.

Sure, she'd be married to Alex. But she couldn't forget the arrangement—it was a marriage of convenience. There were conditions attached. He'd seen she needed help, and she knew he needed citizenship. That's all it was. Maybe they would develop a friendship, and maybe—*maybe*—they might fall in love one day, and their marriage could become something more. But what if it didn't? And how could she know for sure he would raise her child as his own like he said he would? She didn't *know* Alex. She'd been good at reading people, but she couldn't read him. She couldn't tell what was a lie or what was the truth.

And while she'd sat on her bedroom floor, feeling lonelier than she'd ever felt before, she'd cried. She'd cried for her mammy. She'd cried for her daddy and Colleen. She'd cried for her baby—for herself.

And she'd cried for Alex.

It had felt so real, so sure, being in his arms, feeling his lips on hers. But it was an act—nothing more. And now, he would be waiting for her at the inn, waiting to hear whether or not her daddy approved. And she wasn't sure she could look him in the eyes without feeling what she did last night and wondering what the hell she'd gotten herself into.

She breathed in the crisp air, tugging her coat tighter around her and walked to her car. She didn't get a day off work—not really. She worked as the inn needed, at least dropping in for a while each day to make sure everything was going all right. She considered the promotion Alex gave her. Sure, she'd be doing exactly what she had been doing for months. But at least she would be getting paid better and have the proper title. Alex appreciated the work she did at the inn. He knew as much as she did that the inn couldn't survive without her. So, maybe there was some hope for them after all. But she couldn't let herself get excited about it. If she had no expectations, then she wouldn't be disappointed.

Her drive to work did little to calm the nerves that made her nauseous. At least, she thought it was her nerves. It could very well be morning sickness. How soon into the pregnancy should she get morning sickness? She'd have to be at least six weeks along by now. She wasn't sure how the dates were worked out exactly, but that was when it happened.

She was almost surprised Alex wasn't outside working on the inn. Then again, she did recall him saying something about starting work inside the inn. But when she stepped inside, he was nowhere to be seen. She let out a sigh, walking behind the front desk, glancing at the bookings book. One booking for the night. God, she hoped Alex had a plan to save the inn, because at this rate, they were going to have a tough time bringing people in. She supposed that was probably her job. She mentally added trying to work out marketing tactics to her list of things to do.

'Aye, didn't hear ye come in, lass.'

'Morning, Ailbe,' she said.

'Mr Carter was wantin' to see ye when ye got 'ere,' he said, his expression curious. ''ave ye been to see him?'

'I was just looking for him, actually,' she mumbled. She heard a noise upstairs—a rumbling, like something being dragged across the floor. 'Any idea where he might be?'

She heard the noise again, this time louder as though it was something heavier. She glanced up at the roof above her, wondering if something was going to fall through.

'I'd say that's a clue, lass,' Ailbe said, heading into the kitchen.

Hearing the noise a third time made her brow crinkle. 'What the *hell* is going on up there?' she said, more to herself since Ailbe had already left the room.

She climbed the stairs to where the rooms were, finding the one directly above where the front desk was. She poked her head through the open door to find Alex shifting all the furniture to the side of the room. At one end of the room, an old sheet was laid on the floor, and different shades of paint were slapped on the wall next to each other—a pale grey, a beige, a light green, and a very pale lavender that was almost grey.

'What's happening in here?' she asked, stepping carefully inside.

'Oh, good, you're here,' he said, a smile on his face. 'I need your help with something.' He walked towards the wall with the paint on it. 'Which one do you think would look good for the rooms?'

'Aren't you the painter?' She raised an eyebrow.

He shrugged. 'You know more about the inn than I do,' he said. 'Besides, I might pick one you don't like.'

She squinted. 'Why does my opinion matter?'

A coy smile tugged at his lips. 'Well you *are* the

manager,' he said. 'And you'd know what would be more attractive to our guests.'

The gesture warmed her. She'd felt touched that he actually wanted her opinion on the renovations. And hearing him say *our guests* made her heart flutter. Had he started to think of them as an *us*? Did she kind of hope he did?

'Brigid?'

His voice prompted her out of her thoughts. She hadn't noticed she'd been staring at him, lost in her thoughts for longer than what should be normal.

'Umm,' she stammered, trying to clear her thoughts. She focussed on the colours. 'The lavender,' she said. 'It's warm enough to be comfortable, but close enough to grey to be neutral. It'll also go well with some brighter colours in the room.' His smile broadened, her brow furrowing in return. 'What?'

He shook his head. 'It's just that's the one I was leaning towards. I was hoping you'd like it.'

She felt her shoulders relax a little, not realising she'd been tense. 'So, you didn't *really* need me, after all.'

'Oh, but I do,' he said, winking at her. She felt her shoulders tense again, not knowing why.

He tapped his foot on the floor. 'You know, these floorboards aren't too shabby. Can't say the same for the other rooms though,' he said. 'I was thinking we could work at restoring the ones that were still in good condition and replacing the ones that are worse for wear. We can swap them around to make sure the change isn't obvious. It'll be easy enough when we pull them up. But that'll be a while away still.'

Pull them up? 'Wait, why would we pull them up if they're still good?' she asked.

'To put the heating in, of course.'

'What's wrong with the heating we've got?'

He looked over at the furnace on the wall. 'Well, it's ancient for starters,' he said. 'They don't even make them like that anymore. Besides, floor heating would be more efficient and less of a fire hazard.'

'We don't have the money to cover that,' she said, thinking about the inn's funds. Already, everything he'd done would almost blow the budget. With no money being withdrawn, she figured he must have been using his own for now, but it was only a matter of time before he needed more than he had. More than *they* had.

He walked over to her, placing his hands on her shoulders, rubbing them up and down. 'Let me worry about that, love.'

It was then she noticed the heaviness in his eyes, mixed with a caffeinated buzz. She noticed the large coffee cup in the corner, before running her gaze over his body. If she hadn't felt tense herself, maybe she wouldn't have noticed his body was tense while he looked and sounded weary.

'Did you get *any* sleep, Alex?' Her tone had sounded more concerned than she meant.

'Ahh.' He considered her words. 'No, I don't think so. I couldn't stop … thinking.' He reached down and held her hand, shooting warmth up her arm and into her chest. 'What did your daddy say?'

'I don't think he was fully convinced,' she said, trying not to lean closer towards him, even when she tangled his fingers with hers. 'But I think I put his mind at ease.'

'What did you say?'

'I told him I was happy with you.'

His brow creased a little as he searched her eyes. She wanted to reach out and smooth the lines, to kiss him again like they kissed last night, but this time with no one looking. But she had to remind herself of the terms of their arrangement. They were to be married without all the married things—without the feelings. She was just romanticising.

'Are you?' he asked, his voice low.

She tugged her hand free and took a step back. She had work she had to get to and she knew that the longer she stood in such a close vicinity to Alex, the more likely she would make a fool of herself and the harder it would be to resist him.

'I'm appreciative of what you're doing Alex,' she said. 'And I'm relieved that this ... arrangement ... will solve my—our—problems. But happy? It's—' she let a breath out, trying to relax. 'It's something else, don't you think?'

He stood up straighter, his head slightly leaning back so his eyes weren't looking at her anymore, but over her. She'd felt her chest tighten. Had she seen a flicker of hurt cross his face before a wall shot up between them?

'Yeah, something else,' he mumbled. He turned back into the room, finding the can of lavender paint and his paintbrush. She felt as though she couldn't summon her feet to leave—or move at all, for that matter. She didn't even know what to say. He cleared his throat, shaking her out of her thoughts. 'Whether or not he approves, he's going to have to get used to it,' he said, slapping some paint on the wall. He didn't turn to look at her. 'Because we're getting married. On Friday, to be exact.'

Wait, *what*? 'Friday?'

'That's right,' he said, continuing to paint. 'I've already got the license.'

She shook her head. '*Friday*?' she repeated. 'When were you going to tell me, Alex?'

He shrugged. 'I've told you now, haven't I? Turns out a pregnancy *is* still considered a special consideration for getting married quickly. If you weren't pregnant, we would have had to wait for at least a month.'

She felt her blood chill. 'Wait, you didn't get the license in Kinsale did you?' God, everyone would know. And her daddy …

'Of course not,' he said, finally looking at her. His expression was more annoyed than anything. 'Kinsale is obviously the kind of place where people talk—small towns always are. I got it in Cork. We'll be getting married there.'

She breathed a sigh of relief. 'Good.'

'Like I said, Brigid, you don't have to worry,' he said. 'I've got this.'

He returned back to his painting. She took it as a sign that she'd been dismissed, but when she'd left the room and stood looking up and down the hallway, she backtracked into the room, annoyance threading her own voice.

'Why are you working on this room?' she said. 'This is already the best kept room in the inn—it's the only one we can actually charge full price for. Isn't the plan to start on the worst one first?'

He shrugged, keeping his focus on the smooth movements of his hand. 'I was making it up for you,' he said. 'After all, I can't have my *wife* staying in a room that could crumble around her.'

His response surprised her. The way he glanced at her when he called her his wife sent chills to her bones. She swallowed, leaving the room when he'd refocussed on his painting. He'd been considerate enough to make up a room especially for her—all because she'd thrown in the condition that she needed her own room. If he hadn't been so cold in there, she would have thought it had been quite a caring gesture. But she knew the exact moment his tone towards her changed. And she was starting to think she hadn't said the right thing.

***

She wasn't happy with their arrangement. She was grateful she wouldn't be left in the lurch having to fend for herself without anyone to help her. But she wasn't *happy*. Sure, it was all still new. They'd only known each other for a week, and they'd be married on Friday. Of course, he couldn't expect she'd be throwing herself at him, confessing undying love and eternal happiness with him. Heck, she was probably freaking out about the whole arrangement and is just being cautious. She barely knew him, and the only things he knew about her came from people other than herself.

But at the least, he'd expected she would be *happy* going into the arrangement. He'd been a gentleman. He'd done everything right—well, as good as it could be considering the circumstances. He'd jumped through the hoops, trying to impress her father, her friends. Her. He was taking precautions. He'd promised her she wouldn't have to worry about anything—that he would look after her and her child. He was making up a room for her because she'd requested to have a room of her own. And whether or not she believed him when he said it, he *did* feel they would fall in love. It might be a week from now, or it could be months—years, even—but he knew there was a spot for Brigid in his heart. They just had to find it—together.

Alex focussed on his brush strokes, watching as the pale lavender paint smoothed over the aged cream that was spattered with all kinds of suspicious stains. Before he knew it, he'd gone around the whole room and was painting away the last bit of cream on the room. He took a step back once he was finished and let out a breath. The lavender was definitely an improvement and, like Brigid said, it would tie in nicely with some brighter colours throughout the room. Maybe he'd take her with him to pick out the sheets, blankets, and pillows. She looked like the kind of woman who had a keen eye for detail. He felt his body tense as he heard a throat clear, a gruff sound. He turned to face the man who would be his new father-in-law.

'Well, I have to admit,' he said. 'It *is* looking a bit better than what it was. Ailbe said I could find you up here.'

Alex wasn't sure what he should say, or even *if* he should say anything. There was only one thing he could think of: why the hell was Brigid's daddy at the inn? And why the hell was he looking for him? Alex placed the paint and the paintbrush on the floor, covering the leftover paint with a lid, and looked back at Mr Murphy who hadn't moved.

'Did you have something you wanted to talk to me about?' he prompted.

'I still don't trust you.' Alex felt his skin prick. Didn't Brigid say she'd eased his concerns? 'But since Brigid is so … determined … to go through with this, I'll make a deal with you.'

Alex raised his eyebrow. A deal? His mind went into overdrive. Was he going to try to pay him off? Did he want Alex to leave Brigid and never return?

'I'll give you my approval—for now,' Mr Murphy continued, stepping closer to Alex. 'But if I find out you're playing Brigid or have some kind of ulterior motive for marrying her, then all I have to do is make a few phone calls and your visa will be suspended and your citizenship revoked. If you don't treat her right, Alex, you'll be gone before you can blink an eye. Do you understand what I'm saying?'

Mr Murphy was standing so close that Alex might have felt intimidated had he not been built the way he was. Truth is, Alex didn't get intimidated by anyone. But something in the way Mr Murphy spoke made his hairs stand on edge and beads of sweat form on his forehead. Sure, he'd given his approval—barely. But Alex didn't much like the idea of having to watch his back for the rest of his life. He did his best to keep his cool. He knew Brigid's daddy was trying to coax a reaction out of him, but he wasn't going to give him the satisfaction.

'That sounds more like a threat than a deal,' Alex said.

'Call it what you want,' Mr Murphy said. 'But it is what it is.'

'I know you don't particularly like me, Mr Murphy,' he said, not losing eye contact—he had to know he wasn't the only one who was strong enough to stand his ground. 'But I am not going to leave her, and I wouldn't even dream of hurting her. I've already told her she'll never have to worry about anything, and now I'm telling you. I am marrying Brigid.' He spread his arms out. 'It's what we both want. So, you can support us with our decision or not. But I know Brigid wouldn't be happy to find out her daddy was making threats to her fiancé.'

He watched the tiny muscles around Mr Murphy's eyes twitch, his jaw clenched. Alex tried to keep his demeanour as relaxed as possible. If Mr Murphy saw even a hint of him being standoffish, then all his hard work would have been for nothing. Finally, he took a step back from Alex, shaking his finger between them.

'Remember our deal, Alex.'

Threat, Alex thought, wanting to correct him but keeping his mouth shut. He let out a breath of relief once he was certain Mr Murphy had left the inn, bending over with his hands resting on his knees. What the *hell* had he gotten himself into? Had he been rash in proposing to Brigid? Maybe he should have given it some more time and scoped out anything that could go wrong instead of biting off more than he could chew. But he had no time. *They* had no time. Brigid needed this as much as he did— potentially even more. And if it wasn't with him, it would be with someone else. When he'd come here, he had nothing to lose and the world to gain. But now he had Brigid and this inn—the two things he was starting to feel like he'd wasted his life trying to find. And if he got on Mr Murphy's bad side, he could lose it all. So, he had no choice but to dive right in.

Chapter 10

'Are you ready for this?'

He barely recognised his own voice as he gave Brigid's shoulders a gentle squeeze, whispering into her ear. Her hair was pulled into a messy bun, exposing her slender neck, making his body tense. He felt a groan from deep within and he wondered how long he could *really* resist this beautiful woman who had agreed to become his wife—convenience or not. He could feel his warm breath bouncing off the skin of her neck and desperately wanted to feel his lips against her bare skin, tasting her, leaving a trail of kisses and nips. But he pulled himself back before he could, trying his best to resist the temptation. He felt her body shudder as she released a shaky breath.

'Alex, I still don't get why I had to wear a

blindfold,' she said. He thought he could pick up on the nervous tones as she spoke, tugging at something in his chest. 'I've seen you working on it. It's not like it's a *total* surprise.'

A smile tugged at his lips. Honestly, the blindfold was partially because he'd thought she'd look sexy in it—she was. But it was also a trust-building exercise he'd thought of. If she was blindfolded, she *had* to let him lead her up the stairs to the room. She *had* to trust him to not let her stumble. But mostly, it was the sexy thing.

'But you've never seen it finished,' he said.

When had his voice started to sound smooth? He was showing her the room she would be staying in—without him—not trying to seduce her. Even if he wouldn't mind laying her down on the bed and taking all of her and giving her all of him. He cleared his throat, tugging on the red silk that was acting as a blindfold until it came loose and tucking the material into his pocket.

'Your room, my dear.'

He leaned against the doorframe, watching as Brigid fluttered her eyes open, and took in the room. She scanned the room, walking a path to each corner, running her fingers along the bedding and brushing the curtains aside to see outside. He wanted to slide his hand behind her waist and show her through the room himself, but he also couldn't forget their arrangement. Brigid wanted a room to herself for a reason, and it wasn't just because she didn't want to sleep with him. She didn't want to be close to him. She would act the part while they were in public, but behind closed doors, it was just an arrangement. For now.

'Alex, it's—'

'It's not finished,' he said. 'Well, it pretty much is. We just need to put in the heating and replace the windows. But we'll do the whole inn at once for those.'

'It's beautiful.'

She turned to face him from near the window. He could see her eyes glistening in the stream of sunlight entering the room. He strode towards her— slow deliberate steps—and she moved slowly towards him.

'Of course, you don't have to keep the decorations I picked out,' he said. 'You can do what you want with it, since it's your room.'

'I think this looks nice.'

Slowly, step by step, inch by inch, they were drawing closer together. He plucked a stuffed toy dog from the armchair as he passed it.

'This dog, for example.' He shrugged. 'I'm not sure it goes with the theme.' They were only arm's length away from each other. He held the dog up between them, it's face pointing towards Brigid. He peeked over the dog's head. 'But isn't he cute?' He pursed his lips and rounded his eyes, giving her the best puppy-dog eyes he could muster. She raised an eyebrow. 'But, if you don't like dogs …'

Brigid took the dog from him. 'The dog can stay,' she said, her voice teasing. 'But I think you put it in the wrong spot.'

'Oh?'

She carefully placed the dog in the middle of the bed. 'I think he looks happier on the bed, don't you?'

Alex felt his body stir as she leaned over the bed, her jeans tightening across her ass, and had to snap his gaze to her eyes when she stood, her eyebrows raised, and her lips pursed. *Shoot, she noticed*. He felt his mouth drop open then close, no words coming out.

'Were you checking me out, Mr Carter?' Her lips curved into a mischievous smile, her eyes flashing.

'It's hard not to, Miss Murphy,' he said. *So hard*. He tried to silence his inner self, hoping he wouldn't accidentally say anything stupid, but he was too far gone. There was no doubt about it—Brigid made him lose his mind. Her smile widened. 'I was just thinking.'

'About what?' She crossed her arms across her chest.

His eyes dropped to her cleavage that was exposed as her arms folded. *Damn it*. He tried to take slow, deep breaths to control himself, but her closeness and her … flirting … made it difficult. Then it hit him. The way Brigid tilted her head to the side and fluttered her eyelashes up at him. The way she leaned more on her right leg, her left hip lifted slightly higher. The subtle adjustment of her shirt to deepen her cleavage. The mischievous smile and the ring in her voice. Calling him Mr Carter instead of Alex. Brigid *was* flirting with him.

'Well, my dear,' he said, his voice noticeably deeper than usual. 'I'm not sure you could handle it.'

She squinted. 'I'm sure I could handle anything you throw at me.'

His eyes widened, and he felt the sparks shooting inside him. God, if she kept this up, he would forget the conditions of their arrangement and show her what their marriage could really be like. 'All right,' he said, rubbing her bare arm gently, stepping closer so their bodies were only inches apart. 'I was thinking he's a lucky bastard to get a place on your bed.'

'You're not … jealous … of a toy dog, are you?' Her eyebrow swept into a perfect arc.

He shrugged, squinting, and slipped his hands behind her to rest at the small of her back. 'Maybe a little.' All he needed was one sign from her and he was hers.

Her teasing smile lingered for a moment, then her lips parted. He could feel the warmth of her breath mixing with his. Her eyes were searching his, following the movements of his own. He felt her take a shaky breath, her body tensing underneath his hands. And he would have pulled her in for a kiss if he hadn't noticed the change in her eyes. The playful mischievous look in her eyes turned darker, more serious, concerned. Scared? Her breathing came quicker in sharp shallow breaths. Was Brigid freaking out?

'Four days,' she whispered, pushing back against his hands.

He reluctantly let her go, shaking his head in

confusion. She paced back to the window and turned to face him again. She was *definitely* freaking out.

'*Four days*,' she repeated. 'We only have four more days until the wedding and there's so much we need to do. I—' her eyes widened. 'I need a dress. And flowers. And photographs—are we having those done?' She sat on the end of the bed, her knuckles going white from clenching the frame.

'Brigid,' he said, bending down in front of her, his hands on her shoulders, willing her to bring her gaze up to meet his. 'Do me a favour? Stop freaking out.'

'I need a dress,' she repeated. 'You can't *get* a dress with such little notice. It needs to be fitted and—'

'*Brigid*,' he said. She looked up at him, her body shaking beneath his hands. 'We're *eloping*, not having an elaborate wedding. No one else will be there, just us. You could even wear what you're in now if you want to.'

Her eyes narrowed. 'I am *not* getting married in jeans. Marriage of convenience or not, it is still a wedding.'

He shrugged, releasing her shoulders. 'I'm just making a point, Brigid,' he said, standing. 'I'm just saying you don't have to worry—about anything.' He scanned the room. 'Maybe you could start moving in here so it at least *looks* like you're excited to be marrying me.'

He wasn't about to tell her he'd already organised everything to make their wedding as special as possible—the dress, flowers, cars, a photographer. He knew it was still a wedding and, even if they were eloping, he still wanted her to feel as special as she could. And *he* wanted to make her feel special. He didn't want her to buy those things out of necessity. And he wasn't going to let her in on his surprise. Sure, he felt nervous about the life-changing event that was about to happen. But when something big was coming, he did what he knew worked best—he kept himself busy.

He knew he probably sounded like a jackass. But he wasn't about to have his surprise ruined.

***

He was a jackass. An insensitive, unromantic, cold-hearted jackass. Did he seriously tell her not to worry about it? *And* suggest she get married in what she's wearing? And after the moment they shared …

She'd wanted him to kiss her only moments before—a feeling so strong and compelling she was scared she wouldn't be able to resist him. And then it had dawned on her. They were getting married in four days, and he'd been putting all of his focus into the inn. Sure, it was on setting up the room for her to meet her conditions of their arrangement. But how could he be so calm and collected about the whole thing? Was getting married just not that big of a deal to him?

Granted, it was a marriage of convenience. And she'd pretty much guaranteed she wouldn't sleep with him. So, *really*, it's not like he had much to look forward to. Except citizenship. And the inn. And a wife who won't sleep with him and a child that wasn't his.

Oh, God. What had she done?

She'd been clutching at straws, and Alex's offer was one she couldn't refuse. And as much as she tried to convince herself that he needed this arrangement as much as he did, she still felt as though she got the better end of the bargain. Why should Alex care about what happens to the inn? He'd never known Carrick Fitzpatrick. And any time she thought he might actually care about her, it ended with something like this. Him, being cold, coming across as though he didn't give a damn. And her, being confused, scared of those feelings that have been developing ever since ... well, ever since she started to get to know Alex.

Her first impression of him was undesirable. She'd thought she knew his type—she thought she knew *what* type he was. But he kept surprising her. For starters, he didn't have to ask her to marry him. He could have asked anyone who would have been able to give him a better life than she could. He didn't have to focus on renovating the best room at the inn so she could move in, all because she threw in that stupid condition—the one she was starting to regret as she found it harder and harder to resist him. He didn't have to play the part for her daddy.

But he did.

He did all of those things and more.

He cared about the inn she held so close to her

heart, and he did that *before* they got involved. He'd been nothing but a gentleman to her. And she knew she should listen to him and not worry about anything because, among the little she did know about him, she could tell he was a man of his word. But on the other hand, she couldn't read him. It could all be an act—she'd seen how good an actor he could be when he met her daddy. For all she knew, he could be a serial killer who marries all his victims and she was the next in line. But there was something about him—away from the coldness, confusion, and mystery—that made her feel safe when she was with him.

So, like a possessed bride who had one thing on her mind, she went in search of possibly the most important thing she would need for a wedding—a dress. She could probably manage with no flowers or handpicked ones, even. As for photographs—that's what phones were for, right? They could take decent photos nowadays. But Brigid sure as hell wasn't getting married in jeans and a T-shirt. She climbed out of her car and beelined towards the only place in town that sold grossly overpriced dresses for such an occasion—close enough to the port to be off the main drag, and far enough away to not be recognised.

She glanced towards the port, pausing in front of the window of the shop. Many of the fishing boats were out to sea, but there were still the usual port workers plodding along and the self-proclaimed fishermen sitting on the edge with a rod in their hands. She turned back to the shop and pressed her hands to the window, feeling her mouth drop open.

There it was.

Brigid didn't like to do much shopping, especially for something she would only wear once. But this dress? Sure, it was white. But it was fitting to the hips and flowed down into an airy skirt down to the knees. Adorned with a suitable belt or jewellery, the dress could be perfect for near on *any* occasion—particularly, a wedding. And it fit that mannequin perfectly. Her breath catching, she didn't waste any more time gawking at it, pushing inside the shop, and weaving in and out of racks and boxes to get to the mannequin in the window, checking the tag as soon as she reached it. It was her size. And not the most overpriced item she'd ever bought.

She started tugging at the dress, pulling it over the top of the mannequin and cradling it in her arms—the soft fabric felt even better than it looked. She turned to take the dress to the counter and froze, her hairs standing on end and a shiver running down her spine. *Darcy*.

'What are you doing here?'

Should she be trying to hide the dress? But it wasn't a wedding dress, just a really nice white dress. He wouldn't know what it's for, would he?

'How'd you do it, Brig?' His smirk was more wicked than anything. She felt her skin pricking.

'I don't know what you're talking about,' she muttered, trying to squeeze past him with the dress, but he blocked her way.

'Oh, I think you do,' he said, stepping closer towards her, pushing her back against one of the clothes racks. She was surprised it hadn't fallen over. 'Conning the new hot-shot owner of the inn into marrying you.' He clicked his tongue, shaking his head.

'Wait, how did he know they were getting married?

'Did you say *it's* his?' He jabbed a finger against her stomach, forcing a gasp from her mouth. She tightened her lips. Every one of her nerve endings might be on edge, but she refused to give him the satisfaction of scaring her. 'But of course, that would mean you slept with him before he even got here and that really is a new low for you.' He let out a laugh that sounded maniacal. 'So, tell me, Brigid, how did you manage to convince that stupid son of a bitch into agreeing to marry you? Does he even *know* about the child?'

'That's *none* of your business,' she spat at him, her blood boiling. She was putting on a good front— at least, she thought she was—but the truth is, Darcy was terrifying her, and she couldn't see even a slither of the man she'd thought she'd loved. If anything, it was an infatuation with having the idea of him forced upon her for so long.

'Funny, I remember telling your *fiancé* something similar when we first met,' he said, pressing against her again, his face close, his lips curled into a snarl. 'He obviously didn't take any notice either.' She could feel the heat of his breath against the skin of her face, smelling of liquor and mint—as it always had. The very smell disgusted her. 'See, Brigid, it's *my* child. So, as far as I see it, it *is* my business.'

She narrowed her eyes, steadying her voice as much as she could. 'You gave up the right to give a damn when you turned us away, Darcy.'

She felt his finger press harder against her stomach, and she fought a cringe. 'I'll tell you one more time, Brigid. Get. Rid. Of. It.' He ended the sentence on a growl.

'Oh, sorry to interrupt but—are you all right, love?'

Darcy gave Brigid another hard look, as if reinforcing his threat, before he flashed the sweetest smile he could muster and turned towards the elderly lady who owned the shop. Darcy was a lot of things. But he wasn't stupid. If he was to do anything to her, it wouldn't be with witnesses in sight. Brigid looked up at the lady, cringing at the concern on her face.

'It seems she's found a dress she likes,' Darcy said. 'Why don't you ring it up for her? In fact,' he turned towards Brigid. 'I'll pay for it. Consider it a wedding present ... in good faith.'

'It's not my size,' Brigid said. No way in hell was she going to let Darcy have something else to hang over her. Besides, getting married in jeans was starting to sound pretty good right now. She'd wear *anything* to get married in as long as Darcy had nothing to do with it.

'Oh, but I know that dress, dear,' the lady said.

'And you would look like perfection in it.'

She shrugged. 'I changed my mind, sorry.' It wasn't a complete lie—Darcy's appearance had tainted her opinion of the dress, of everything.

'Shame,' the lady said.

'Get the dress, Brigid,' Darcy growled, the sweet smile still plastered on his face. Talk about two-faced … 'You would hate to think of this nice lady starving because she couldn't make a sale, would you?'

She glanced out the window towards her car and a thought occurred to her. She pulled the most convincing smile she could. 'All right,' she said. 'Since you're offering.'

Admittedly, the smile on the lady's face made her feel a warmth inside of her. Darcy was probably right on this—she probably needed the sale. So, while she told them the tally and Darcy pulled out his card, Brigid asked if she could pick it up on Friday. The lady was hesitant.

'There would be a holding fee,' she said. 'But I can keep it out the back for you.'

'Oh, money's not a problem, right, Darcy?' she said, turning to Darcy. His eyes were wild, scolding, seething. Then, he nodded.

'Right.'

Darcy paid for the dress and as they stepped outside, she backtracked. 'I forgot to ask her what time I can pick it up,' she lied, holding up her hand. 'You don't need to wait. I have to rush back to work. But thank you for the dress, Darcy.'

'Remember what I said, Brigid!' he called after

her.

She glanced through the door as she closed it behind her, watching him straighten his jacket and greeting some people who were walking past. Taking a deep breath, she beelined for the register where the lady still stood, wrapping the dress.

'Sorry,' she said, placing her hand on the dress. 'But I really have changed my mind about the dress.'

The lady's face dropped. 'Oh.'

'But please, keep the money,' she said. 'For the inconvenience this has caused. Just—' she paused, swallowing. 'Please don't put the dress in the window again.'

The lady nodded, as if understanding Brigid's hidden meaning. 'All right,' she said. 'Thank you, dear.'

Brigid smiled. 'You're welcome.' She started heading out of the shop, relieved that Darcy had moved on and wouldn't be bothering her anymore. Her hand was on the doorknob when she heard the lady's voice.

'I hope he's better than him,' she said timidly. 'The man you're marrying.'

She took a deep breath, turning her head slightly, a smile creeping across her face. 'He is.'

She knew he was.

Chapter 11

'I can't believe we're actually doing this.'

Alex glanced over at the passenger seat. Brigid was staring out the side window, wrangling her hands in her lap. He didn't know about her, but the last few days had been the longest days of his life. Was it from excitement? Nerves? Fear? He couldn't quite be sure. But he was sure of one thing—he was looking forward to the next part of their adventure, regardless of where it took them. If anyone told him two weeks ago that he'd find a girl and marry her within the first couple of weeks of moving to Kinsale, he would have laughed in their face. Especially after Betty.

He'd had one thing on his mind when he moved—a distraction. The inn was that distraction.

He didn't plan on finding a woman. Sure, if, by some kind of miracle, he managed to make the inn successful in the small amount of time he had and decided to stay, he was sure he'd find a woman one day. But here he was, driving to Cork, his fiancée—who he'd met a week and a half ago—by his side, in a situation that didn't follow the norm. Heck, he'd never even imagined he'd marry someone without knowing them. But somehow, somewhere in those first few days of meeting Brigid, he'd lost all sense of rationality and thought that marrying her would be a good idea. And, as stupid as it sounded, he was still convinced it was.

Brigid did that to him.

She didn't know what kind of an effect she had on him. But the way her eyes could go from soothing to wild in a matter of seconds, and how her demeanour could go from being passionate and fiery to timid had him on his toes. He was sure this woman was the strongest woman he'd ever met. She was independent, fiery, knew what she wanted and wasn't afraid to ask for it. She didn't need protecting. But when her auburn curls draped softly over her shoulders like they were doing now, hiding half of her face, and her hands twisted nervously, her body tense, he couldn't fight the urge to make her feel safe, protected, comforted. Even if their marriage was an arrangement.

He reached towards her, taking one of her hands in his, resting it between them.

'You're not planning on leaving me at the altar,

are you?' he teased.

She glanced up at him, a smile tugging at her lips, and dropped her gaze to their interlocked hands. 'I'm not one to go back on a deal.'

He felt his body flinch. He knew he was the one to propose a marriage of convenience, but referring to it as a deal, or an arrangement, was starting to become uncomfortable.

'Are you going to keep calling it a deal once we're married?'

'I—' she paused, looking up at him, her brow furrowed, confusion flashing across her face. 'But that's what it is, isn't it? An arrangement?'

He shrugged. 'Well, we have to look like we're in love, not signing our lives away.'

She scoffed. 'That would be easier to do if we actually *were* in love.'

'I don't think it would be too hard.' Especially since he was already halfway there. But he wasn't about to admit that to her. If there was one thing he learned from relationships, it was to not jump in too quickly. But it was a bit late for that now.

'Don't you feel like this is crazy?' she said. 'Who gets married without even knowing the person?'

He tilted his head from side to side before glancing over at her again. 'Lots of people, I'd imagine.'

They drove in silence for a few more minutes, Alex stealing glances when he could. Her brow was furrowed, and he was sure her mouth opened and closed a few times. The worried look on her face tugged at his heart, but he knew better than to press her. She'd been off since he showed her the finished room and said it was hers. She didn't even want help moving her things into her room. Sure, she didn't actually have much to move, but he had still noticed her off mood. He tried to put it down to nerves and her pregnancy—he'd heard women can have mood swings while they're pregnant. Maybe it was a good thing she was staying in her own room.

'Alex?' she said timidly.

'Yes, sweetheart?' He glanced over just in time to see the fire flicker in her eyes again. He smiled. He was sure he liked the fiery Brigid better, but felt a pang of disappointment when she pulled her hand away from his.

'You realise Cork is only about half an hour away from Kinsale, right?'

He nodded.

'And we're getting married tomorrow, right?'

'That's right.'

She turned in her seat so she was facing him. 'So, why the hell are we going there today? And why did you tell me to pack a bag?'

He couldn't hold the smile back, but he tried his best. 'A few reasons.'

'Like?'

'Like errands, for starters. I've got to pick up a few things.'

'And?'

'I figured I'd like to spoil my bride a little before we get married.'

He glanced at her again, just in time to see her covering the blush in her cheeks with her hands. 'You do realise this is a marriage of *convenience*, right?'

He shrugged, flashing her a toothy smile. 'There's no harm in having a little fun.'

'Well, that depends on what you mean by *fun*.'

'Dinner,' he said, tilting his head. 'Maybe a walk. Who knows? If you're lucky, I might kiss you again.'

'If *I'm* lucky?' She scoffed. 'I think it should be if *you're* lucky.' She slapped him playfully on the arm.

'Oh, come on,' he teased. 'I know you haven't stopped thinking about that kiss.'

'What makes you so sure?' Her voice hit a pitch higher than what was usual for her, and he knew he'd caught her out. *She* knew he'd caught her out.

'Because I haven't.'

When he didn't get a response, he looked over at her. Her jaw was slack, her mouth open slightly, her eyes studying him as if trying to determine whether or not he was serious. He pulled the car in front of the hotel he'd booked them in at and turned to face her.

'Really?' she whispered, something in her eyes he hadn't seen there before. Something soft, uncertain, flattered. Had he done it? Had he actually flattered the elusive Brigid?

'Really.'

***

She'd been so close to telling him about the whole

dress thing with Darcy. Over the last few days, the car ride to Cork, any time she'd been near him and any time she'd been by herself, she'd wanted to tell him. But, how could she? How could she tell the man she was set to marry tomorrow that her ex had threatened her? How could she tell him she jumped every time she was by herself and heard a noise? How could she tell him she felt like there was someone watching—*always* watching—even when she knew it couldn't be possible? How could she tell him she felt like her life was in danger?

She'd taken no time moving her things—done and dusted in a day. She'd spent the last few nights in her room at the inn. God, even just being down the hall from Alex made her feel safer, though still strangely alone. She'd caught a few glimpses of Darcy down the street. And he'd seen her. He'd given her a look each time which sent a shiver down her spine. And each time he gave her that look, he'd tapped his watch. He was planning something, she knew he was. But she couldn't tell anyone.

Why?

Because no one would believe her.

Darcy had credibility. He had a persona, a high standing. A rapport with everyone important. Brigid had nothing. Her daddy was well-respected, but Brigid was a disappointment. She worked in a run-down inn, never following her daddy's suggestions for her life, forging her own path. Everyone knew that. She had no one, except for Alex. And if she told him, he would think she was crazy. So, the only thing she could do was make sure she was never alone, which was hard to do when she had a room of her own at the inn. Sleep hadn't been coming easy the last few nights. But maybe here, in her own room in Cork, she could. Surely, Darcy wouldn't have followed her here. No one knew where they were going. No one knew *where* they were getting married.

But a part of her still wished Alex hadn't booked two rooms for them—one each. It was her condition of their marriage. But that was before Darcy had threatened her on Monday. But she couldn't expect Alex to agree to sleep in the same room as her without sleeping *with* her. She hoped she was worried for no reason. Why should she think Darcy could actually do anything to her? He couldn't possibly be *that* crazy.

Brigid checked the time on the alarm clock near her hotel bed. Alex had checked them in and told her he'd be back in a couple of hours to pick her up for their date. He said he had some errands to run, but she did wonder why she couldn't join him. She could have looked through the shops, got coffee, or done anything other than sitting in her room watching the clock. Sure, the long bath she'd allowed herself had been needed—she couldn't remember the last time she'd had a bath. She'd taken time to do her hair and makeup and dressed in the one dress she'd brought with her. She had planned to wear it for their wedding, even though it was a pale blue, but she also hadn't expected that Alex wanted to take her out for dinner and she couldn't dress casually to a night out in Cork. She knew she should have packed more than one dress.

Her body jumped when she heard a knock on the door. Even though she knew it would have to be Alex, she couldn't be too sure. She looked through the peephole, relieved it was him. She scolded herself for being so jumpy. But maybe that's what Darcy's plan was. Maybe he didn't plan on *doing* anything to her but having her living her life looking over her shoulder was enough for him. She took a breath. She wouldn't give him that satisfaction. She couldn't let him think he'd won. She had to get the jumpiness under control.

She straightened her dress and opened the door, flashing a smile at Alex. He was wearing neat dark jeans and a long-sleeved buttoned shirt with the top two buttons undone and the sleeves rolled up to just below his elbows. He smelled clean, crisp, a mixture of lemon-scented soap and spice. And the very sight of him made her insides push against her skin as though trying to urge them closer. He had a suit bag draped over his shoulder, though it looked too thick to be a suit. She watched as his eyes scanned her from head to toe and back up to her eyes.

'Brigid, you look, ahh—'

'This was all I had,' she said tentatively.

'Incredible,' he finished. 'You look beautiful.'

He leaned forward, sweeping a quick kiss on her cheek, and walking past her into her room. She closed the door behind him but didn't follow him.

She just watched as he scanned the room and walked straight towards the wardrobe, opening it up and hanging the suit bag carefully.

'You're not trying to smuggle something in that bag, are you?' she teased. She crossed her arms and leaned back against the bench of the little kitchenette.

His eyes flashed, and his smile made her relieved that she was already leaning against something for support. 'Just a dress,' he said. He scrunched his nose. 'I'm pretty sure it's not illegal.'

Her mouth dropped open. 'A dress? What for?'

'For you, of course,' he said, closing the wardrobe door. 'A little birdy told me you were getting married.'

Her mind ticking with questions, she didn't notice her feet closing the distance between them, moving her closer to the dress. 'Let me see it.'

He leaned against the wardrobe door, spreading his arms out as if guarding it. 'No, you can't.'

His eyes were still flashing, and her feet came to a stop in front of him. She tried to reach around him for the doorhandle, but he kept brushing her hand away.

'Oh, come on,' she said. 'Why can't I see it?'

'Because, Miss Murphy, you can't see it until your wedding day,' he said, matter-of-factly. 'And that's *tomorrow*.'

'The *groom* is the one who's not supposed to see the dress until the wedding day.' She tried to act annoyed, but she was sure her amusement was showing through. He'd bought her a dress? But not just any dress—a *wedding* dress. And he'd bought it. For her. And the bastard could have saved her a whole lot of stress and worry—not to mention bumping into Darcy—if he'd just told her he had it sorted.

But he had.

He'd told her not to worry about anything. And she didn't listen. She thought he was being insensitive, but he'd already had it sorted. She remembered he'd gone to Cork last week—that must have been when he organised the dress. Before the dinner with her daddy. He was already certain then.

'But I've already seen it,' he said. 'So, you're not allowed to see it.'

'It doesn't work that way, Alex.' She smiled. Admittedly, it was a very sweet gesture. And he looked adorable. Maybe if she could distract him long enough to get between him and the wardrobe …

'Well, we are doing everything in this relationship backwards, Brigid,' he teased.

She flipped her hair over her shoulder, puffed her chest out a little—she knew her cleavage looked good in this dress—and pouted, running her fingertips from his chest down to his stomach, almost surprising herself. *Damn*, he had some abs. 'Not even a little peek?' she asked in a sweet voice.

His eyes followed her hands trailing down his body, up to her cleavage, and to her pout. She was sure she saw his jaw twitch. She fluttered her eyes at him, tilting her head into her shoulder. And for a moment, she got lost in him. His hands smoothed down her back, stopping at her hips. He squeezed them gently, tugging her closer to him, and moved his lips against her cheek, barely touching. It sent a shiver down her spine, and briefly, she'd forgotten the real reason why she was trying to seduce him.

***

He knew exactly what she was trying to do. Admittedly, it took him a moment to work it out. The way she touched him with those deliciously naughty fingertips, fluttered those gorgeous green eyes up at him, and pressed her body closer towards him would make any man's mind blank. Sure, he had expected she would be curious about the dress and want to see it. In fact, there really was no stopping her once they were back from their dinner. But he couldn't resist teasing her. God, if he knew she was going to try to seduce him just to see the dress, he would have brought it back with him last week.

But as much as he'd love to see just how far she would go with her seducing, they had a reservation at the most recommended seafood restaurant in Cork they were going to be late to. But what was a few more minutes? After all, two could play at her game.

He gave her hips another squeeze, moving his parted lips across her jawline, feeling his warm breath mingling with the heat of her body. He moved his hand up her back, tangling in her hair, tugging gently to the side to expose her neck a little more. He heard her soft moan as he gently touched his lips to her collarbone, nipping lightly enough to not mark her. She pressed her body further into him—the slightest of movements. It almost sent him over the edge. If he didn't stop now, there was no stopping. He moved his mouth up to her ear, nipping the lobe, grasping his hands around her hips again.

'Oh, *Lolita*,' he whispered, tsking in her ear, feeling her body tense beneath his hands. 'My naughty little minx.'

She tried to pull back, but he was too quick for her. In one swift movement, he tugged her up and swung her over his shoulder, holding her in place by the small of her back, smiling at the little squeal she couldn't stop. He moved them towards the door, her legs kicking and her arms flailing, smacking his ass.

'Put me down, Alex!' she cried between squeals and giggles.

'Not happening,' he said, a smile plastered on his face. 'Not until we're outside.'

Out of the corner of his eyes, he saw her grab her purse from the bench as they walked past.

'You're crazy,' she said.

But the tone of her voice told him she was enjoying it.

Chapter 12

'We're not going in there, are we?'

Alex stepped to the side of the restaurant door to let someone past, looking at Brigid's worried look. 'That was the plan.'

'I, umm …' She hesitated, fiddling with her purse. Her face scrunched up as though she didn't want to say what she was about to. Admittedly, she looked adorable. 'I don't like seafood,' she said quietly.

His eyes widened. 'You live in Kinsale.'

'I know.'

'A *fishing* town.'

She cringed, baring her teeth in an awkward smile. 'Unfortunately.'

'And you don't like seafood?'

She shook her head. 'I can't stand the taste of it.'

He stared at her for a moment, taking her all in. He was aware his mouth had dropped open, and that he probably looked like he was gawking, but this woman kept surprising him—in all the ways. Finally, he closed his mouth, nodded his head, and took her hand in his.

'All right, we'll go somewhere else,' he said, leading them away from the restaurant.

'I'm sorry, Alex,' she muttered, staring at the ground as they walked.

'So, that was a quick date,' he said, nudging her shoulder with his.

'You're not calling it quits because of that, are you?' she said

'Well, I'm not sure I could live a life without seafood,' he teased.

She stopped in her tracks, looking up at him. 'Really? I—'

He pressed his free hand against her face, rubbing his thumb over the mound of her cheek. 'I'm kidding, Brigid,' he said. 'I can live without seafood.' He leaned closer, his mouth near her ear. 'Just don't ask me to give up red meat,' he whispered. He pulled back in time to see the red tinge fading from her cheeks, her eyes flashing.

'Oh, that would be more painful for me than it would for you.'

'Mmm, I'm not sure about that,' he said.

They walked down the street, side by side, in silence, observing passers-by and taking in the crisp night air. He saw Brigid shudder a little and let go of her hand only to pull her close, his arm around her.

'So, anything else I should know?' he asked. 'Other foods you don't eat? Allergies?'

She didn't answer immediately, her brow furrowed and her teeth biting into her bottom lip. 'I'm allergic to anti-inflammatory drugs,' she said. 'And I'll eat anything except seafood. What about you?'

He shook his head. 'Oh, I'm a big fan of food,' he teased, mentally locking away her allergy into the vital information sector of his brain. 'I'll eat almost anything. And I have no allergies.'

She raised an eyebrow. 'What do you mean by *almost* anything?'

He felt his lips tug up to the side. 'Well, Scott told me of this time he tried *escargot*,' he said. 'He recommended against it. And I take his suggestions very seriously.'

'Is Scott one of your friends?' she asked, glancing up at him.

He moved her in front of him to let some people pass them before sliding back into step next to her. They were walking slower than everyone else on the footpath, but he didn't mind. It was actually … nice.

'More like a brother,' he said. 'He's been my best friend for years. His family was like my second family, especially after my dad died. Scott had already moved to Paris, but his parents and his sister were always there for me and were always good for a homecooked meal.'

'Were you close?' she asked hesitantly. 'To his

sister?'

He stopped walking, pulling her into his arms against the wall of one of the shops. People continued to walk past, oblivious of them. In a strange way, it was private.

'If you're asking if you should be worried,' he said, his hands around her waist. She pressed her palms to his chest, stirring something inside of him that made him want to be back in that hotel room with her. 'Then you shouldn't. Liz and I—we're friends. We went on a few dates once before, but it was weird. It was more like we were hanging out as friends. I think she's always been just a little sister to me.'

Her eyes fluttered up at him, a mischievous smile tugging at her lips. 'Now, what makes you think I'd be worried, Mr Carter?'

'Maybe because you'll be my wife tomorrow, Miss Murphy.' He tucked a loose curl behind her ear, letting his thumb linger against her cheek. 'Do you know what you feel like for dinner yet?'

She glanced up at the neon sign flashing above them. 'How do you feel about burgers?'

He smiled. 'From a seafood restaurant to fast food?' He let out a deep breath, shaking his head. 'This date must *really* be going well.'

She grabbed his hand and pulled him towards the door. 'You're right, it *is* a step up, don't you think?'

Before he knew it, she'd pulled him over to a booth and was already ordering two burgers with the lot and extra fries.

***

Okay, maybe she'd been a *little* worried about Liz. He'd seemed so convincing when he said she was more like a sister than anything else. But she still couldn't justify why she had even felt worried about another woman in his life. She'd never thought she'd be the jealous type—like, the super-jealous type who got worked up over simply being friends with another woman. But something told her Liz wasn't the one to be worried about.

'All right,' Alex said, finishing his bite of the burger. 'Soup or stew?'

Brigid was aware they were both grossly overdressed for a burger shop, but she also figured a less formal setting would make a more comfortable date. She smiled. Alex had decided that a good way to get to know each other was to play a game of questions, giving two options, and she would choose which one she preferred.

'Stew. I'm Irish, remember?' she said effortlessly, popping a fry in her mouth. 'You?'

'Stew,' he said, nodding his head. 'As long as it's lamb.'

'Mmm …' Brigid rested her chin on her hand. She could feel Alex's foot pressing against hers and his knee brushing against her leg under the table. She'd be lying if she said she didn't like it. 'Board games, or cards?'

'Oh, nothing beats a good game of cards,' he said.

Her jaw dropped. 'No way!' she said. 'Board games win, hands down.'

'Agree to disagree?' he said, his eyes flashing.

'Just this once,' she said, stealing one of his fries. He picked up her burger and took a bite. 'Hey!'

'What? You started it,' he said, his mouth full. 'On top of the sheets, or under?'

'To sleep?' He winked. 'Under,' she said. 'I freak out if my legs aren't covered while I sleep.'

'What about for … not sleeping?' he teased.

She raised an eyebrow. 'Well, that depends on the position, don't you think?'

His eyes widened, and he started choking, coughing into his arm. He grabbed his glass of water and took a sip, clearing his throat when he finally stopped coughing. 'Are you very skilled in positions, Brigid?'

Not at all, considering she'd only been *with* a man once before, and that turned out to be one of her least enjoyable experiences. But she couldn't fight the thought that it would be a heck of a lot more enjoyable with Alex. She cleared her throat. 'You'll never know.' She took a sip from her water.

'I wouldn't say *never*, right?' he said. She sprayed her mouthful of water into a napkin, surprising herself that it didn't go everywhere and make her look like a fool. 'I mean, we are getting married tomorrow.'

She felt the blush creep across her cheeks. 'Well, maybe *one day*.'

'Sooner or later?' he asked, leaning on his elbows

to be closer. She tilted her head from side to side, trying her best to hide the smile that was pushing through. '*Sooner!*' he said, pushing himself back in his seat, his mouth open with excitement, his eyes teasing. She felt the blush deepen. He shook his head slowly. 'My, my, Brigid. You *are* a naughty little minx, aren't you?'

His grin was mischievous, and there was something in the way he looked at her that made her heart skip a beat and the butterflies start batting against the walls of her stomach. And she realised something—he was right. One day, they might fall in love. Their marriage of convenience might turn into a real marriage. They might have children of their own. They might grow old together, making memories as they go through life, travelling and living. And she would be happy with that. In fact, she would *love* that. And they had all the time in the world. Knowing that that was the future ahead of them made her actually look forward to saying 'I do' tomorrow.

Her eyes widened. She shushed him. 'Keep it down, will you? I don't want everyone to know.'

He studied her for a moment, his eyes flashing, his knee resting against hers, and leaned across the table, taking her hand, and pressing it against his lips. 'Well, I look forward to it.'

'I bet you do,' she teased.

They finished their burgers and ordered a sundae to share, laughing together and playing their game of questions until they couldn't think of anything else to compare.

'So,' Alex started, taking a scoop of ice-cream as soon as the waitress left. 'If you don't mind me asking, what happened with you and Darcy?'

She fiddled with the spoon, contemplating what to say. Of course, she *should* tell him what happened. It was only fair since he was going to be her husband by lunchtime tomorrow. But she hadn't told anyone before. She barely even admitted it to herself.

'It, umm,' she stammered, trying to find the right words. She stared at the spoon twirling between her fingers. 'It wasn't really our idea to start with. Our daddy's sort of … pushed it. The two most respected families in Kinsale—who wouldn't think the union was a good idea?'

She thought she saw a twitch in his jaw like he wanted to say something, but he held back, obviously giving her the chance to talk. She added that to the steadily growing list of things she liked about him.

'I always thought something was off about him,' she continued. 'But I didn't want to disappoint my daddy any more than I already had. We were never in love, but I guess we just fell into habit. He, umm,' she paused, glancing up at him briefly before dropping her gaze back to the spoon. 'He got me drunk, maybe even drugged, I'm not really sure. He … took advantage … of me. It was my, umm …' she cleared her throat before finishing. 'First.'

His eyes widened. 'God, Brigid,' he whispered. She was sure she heard a growl in his voice, but she kept her focus on the spoon.

'Then I was *late*,' she said, fighting back the tears that threatened. 'And I thought that was it—I was going to be stuck with him forever. But it turns out he'd been seeing someone else on the side. Or, I guess, I was the one that was on the side. But he'd already proposed to her before I could tell him I was pregnant. And that's when you came in.'

She found the courage to look at him again. He sat silently, his jaw clenched, his eyes flashing all different shades of red. His hands gripped the edge of the table, his knuckles whiter than a blank sheet of paper.

'Alex?' she said tentatively. 'Please tell me what you're thinking.'

He shook his head slowly, bringing one of his hands up to pinch the bridge of his nose between his eyes. 'I wish I'd punched that son of a bitch harder.'

She let out the breath she'd been holding on to. 'You broke his nose, Alex,' she said. 'He's still sporting the bruise.'

'Like I said,' he continued, his eyes connecting with hers. 'I should have punched him harder.'

She felt a shiver down her spine. His words were cold, hollow, but still, somehow, made her feel warm, protected. The look in his eyes caught her, silently promising that he would always be the one to protect her. And she would let him. *God,* she would let him. None of the men in her life had been anything like Alex. Her daddy had always tried to control her and Colleen. Darcy had been even worse.

Ailbe had been the only man she could trust.

Until now.

'It's your turn,' she whispered, reaching her hand across the table, and placing it on his hand, still clenched on the table. She ran her thumb over his white knuckles until his hand relaxed and the colour came back. He looked at her questioningly. 'There was someone in Paris, wasn't there?' she urged.

He hesitated for a moment and she wondered if he was thinking the same thing she thought when he asked about Darcy. Except his silence lasted half as long as hers did and he never took his eyes off her.

'Her name was Betty,' he said. 'I went to visit Scott in Paris when the place I worked for foreclosed. We met and hit it off.'

'How serious was it?' she asked, holding her breath.

'Enough to stay in Paris for two years.'

Brigid exhaled, unsure of how she felt about it. Two years was a long time to spend with someone, especially if it was serious enough to move to another country to be with them. But then, she couldn't talk. She was pregnant with her ex's child— her ex who'd played her like a fool for years. She hadn't realised she'd dropped her gaze to stare at the empty dessert bowl between them, her hands gripping her glass, until his hand laid on hers.

'It's over, Brigid,' he said, his voice soothing. 'She was cheating on me for months.'

'Did you know?' she asked quietly, looking up at him.

He shook his head. 'I would have been in Kinsale quicker if I knew.' She looked at him questioningly, urging him to go on. He sighed. 'I'd asked her to come with me and she didn't want to. I thought I had time, so I waited a while. But it turned out she was seeing someone else and didn't want to leave because of him.'

'So, it only just happened?'

He nodded slowly.

'You didn't—' she stammered, hesitating. 'I mean, I'm not a … rebound … am I?'

He smiled, a broad smile that made her heart flip. 'Honey, you could never be a rebound.' He ran his thumb over the soft part of her wrist, sending a shiver up her arm and down her spine. 'Besides, when someone does something like that and you realise what you thought was love was actually only infatuation, you don't need anything to help you get over it. I'd say you felt the same with Darcy.'

She nodded. She knew the feeling well. Heartbreak was one thing, but when you realise you'd been played for the entirety of the relationship, it's something completely different. You don't need help getting over them, because you realise they're not worth the worry—that you never *really* had anything with them.

Alex paid the bill for the food and they walked back to the hotel, hand in hand, their fingers wound together, their shoulders bumping. Their walk was in silence, but it didn't feel awkward. It felt … comfortable. Relaxing. In those silent moments, they were just enjoying each other's company. Alex walked her to the door of her room. Brigid turned to face him.

'Would you ever leave me?' she asked.

'That depends,' he said. She felt a momentary pang of disappointment until she saw the flash in his eyes. 'Would you ever cheat on me?'

She smiled, rolling her shoulders flirtatiously. 'Mmm … maybe,' she teased. 'If I could find someone stronger …' She gripped his biceps. 'Sexier …' Her hands moved from his arms to his chest, running her fingertips down his chest. 'Who could offer me a better deal …'

He clutched his hand to his chest. 'Oh, Miss Murphy, how you wound me!'

'Though, I think that might be hard to find,' she continued. 'Do you know of anyone, Mr Carter?'

He rested his hands on her hips, pulling her closer. 'I think maybe my alter-ego could help you out.'

She slid her hands up his chest to rest around the back of his neck, running her fingers through his dark hair. *God*, it did feel as good as it looked—soft, silky.

'I'd like to meet him someday,' she whispered.

'I'm sure I could arrange that.'

He tugged her closer and pressed his lips to hers—sweet, gentle, a caress. She could feel her body swaying slowly with his as she pressed into the kiss, standing on her tip-toes. She felt the tip of his tongue slide against the seam of her lips, and parted her lips to let him in. God, it felt good. It felt … right.

And his taste was addictive and had her craving more of him. She wiggled her body closer to him, eliciting a deep groan from the base of his throat before he broke the kiss, resting his forehead against hers.

'Looks like you got lucky after all,' he teased, his eyes refusing to let go of hers.

'I still think *you're* the one who got lucky,' she said, unable to wipe the stupid smile from her face.

He moved his hand from it's spot on her hip and smacked her on the ass. 'Goodnight, Brigid.' He winked as he pulled away, walking backwards.

She slid the key card into the slot, unlocking the door, and opened it up. 'Goodnight, Alex,' she said. She nudged her way into her room, but before she could close the door, she heard her name being called.

'Brigid?'

She poked her head around the door. Alex had stopped walking, but he was smiling at her.

'*Don't* look at the dress.'

She smiled. When the door was locked, she slid onto the ground, resting her back against the door, the gawkiest smile on her face—she was sure of it.

At this point, she'd do anything he asked her to.

Chapter 13

Brigid ran her fingertips over the beaded bodice of her wedding dress—the beads were a pale blue, adding a hint of colour to her white dress that loosely fit her to her hips and draped down to the floor. The material transformed into a soft lace over her shoulders, the neckline forming a V. A pale blue ribbon matching the beads tied around the waist in a perfect bow at the back. God, Alex picked *this* out? Not only was she about to marry a man thoughtful enough to take care of finding a dress for her, she was marrying one with style. She was glad she'd resisted the urge to look at the dress last night—it made it that much more of a delightful surprise. Granted, she was up early—before sunrise, to be exact. But who wouldn't be awake for half the night before getting married?

She tucked a stray hair into her bridal bun, feeling a flutter of nervousness and excitement when she heard a knock on the door. He was here, ready to take her to promise their lives to each other. And the excitement before getting to the door had her temporarily forgetting it was just a formality. She flung the door open, ready to see Alex, only to find the concierge holding a small bouquet of a variety of white and green flowers, tied at the stems with a ribbon the same blue as the one on her dress. A woman dressed in a skirt-suit stood behind him holding a camera.

'Miss Murphy,' the concierge said. 'Mr Carter has instructed that we escort you to your car.' Wait, *car?* He handed the bouquet to her. 'These are for you. If you don't mind, Ciara would like to take some pre-wedding photos by the mirror in the hallway.'

'Where's Alex?' she asked.

'Mr Carter is already on his way to the venue,' he said.

She took the breath she'd forgotten to take while her mind ran wild. Alex organised *everything*? Flowers, photos, a dress, a *car*? Heck, they were even arriving separately! She tried to regulate her breathing with slow deep breaths and followed the photographer to the mirror. She could see why Alex told her not to worry about anything.

Because he'd already taken care of it all.

***

There were two kinds of late for a bride.

There was fashionably late, being five maybe ten minutes late—the usual kind of late that gives stragglers a chance to get there and everyone to be seated.

Then, there was the late that just kept on going, making everyone wonder if the bride was even going to turn up. Time keeps on ticking, second by second, minute by minute, and people—namely the celebrant—start to try to convince the groom she's not coming.

She was late.

Considering they were eloping, there were no stragglers, and the only people who needed to be there other than the bride were already there. And another thing with eloping, being late is *bad*. With eloping, there is no patience. There's time. And there's back-to-back bookings. There is no *late*.

The celebrant tapped his foot impatiently.

'She'll be here,' Alex said, not entirely convinced himself. 'Just give her a few more minutes.'

'That's what you said half an hour ago, Alex,' the celebrant said. He pointed to a couple who had just walked into the chapel hall. 'My next couple is already here.'

'Please?'

'I'm sorry, Alex,' the celebrant said. 'Your time is *up*.'

Shoot. He tried to come up with an excuse—anything—to explain why Brigid was late, but he couldn't. He was at a complete and total loss. He'd thought that organising everything for Brigid would make sure she got there. He'd done it all right. He'd wanted to make it as special for her as he could, and she didn't even bother to show up. The celebrant ushered him out into the hallway and closed the door, the couple who were on time with him.

'Damn it!'

He sat on one of the seats in the hallway, his elbows on his knees and his head clasped between his hands. His emotions were mixed—angry, frustrated. Sad? And then, he couldn't stop the pathetic laugh that picked the worst time to come. How had he become like this? Being rejected by *two* girls in a matter of weeks.

'God, you *idiot*,' he mumbled.

How could he be fooled into thinking this would work? How had he been so blinded to the fact that he didn't know Brigid? Why had he been so sure …

He heard the door swing open at the end of the hallway and looked up. There she was, in the dress he'd bought her, looking very frazzled, her hair wind-tussled, her feet bare, one hand clutching the straps of her heels, dangling them next to her, her other hand pressed to her side.

She was beautiful.

She was *here*.

And he couldn't move.

'Oh, God, did I miss it?' she said, her voice stressed.

'Only a little,' he said.

She flopped onto the seat next to him, dropping her heels to the floor, letting out an exasperated sigh. She pressed her palms to her eyes, obviously not worried about smudging her makeup.

'I'm sorry, Alex,' she whispered.

'Hey,' he said, nudging his shoulder against hers. She brought her gaze up to meet his. 'You look like hell—'

Her mouth dropped open and she slapped him on the arm. 'Is that how you compliment a bride?'

He smiled. 'But you still look stunning.' He attempted to tuck a curl behind her ear, but it sprung back to its spot next to her eye. 'Hands down, the most beautiful bride I've ever seen.'

She squinted at him. 'Do you mean that?'

'Absolutely.' He took hold of one of her hands and smoothed his thumb over the back of it—small circular movements. 'What happened, Brigid?'

She groaned. 'What *didn't* happen? Everything was going so well. That beautiful old-fashioned car you hired for me—I loved it.' She tilted her head to the side, diverting her gaze to the floor. 'Until it broke down and I had to run a few blocks to get here.'

'Seriously?' The car broke down? After everything he did to make sure this day was special for Brigid, the damn car had to break down.

She nodded. 'I literally *ran*, Alex,' she said. 'In a wedding dress. But *then* ...' She picked up her heels, dangling them in front of Alex. He noticed one of the heels was dangling from the rest of the shoe by a thread. *Shoot*. 'Half a block of running, and my heel breaks. But I still had to get here, right? So, I took my shoes off and walked the rest of the way on a twisted ankle. *And*—oh, God—I left the flowers in the car, too!' She rested her head in her hands. 'God, I'm a mess.'

He placed his hand on her back, rubbing in smooth motions. 'Don't worry about all that, Brigid,' he said. 'You're here now.'

'But we missed our time slot,' she mumbled into her hands.

'So?' She glanced up at him, confusion on her face. He pointed to the door of the room where the celebrant was. 'Whether he wants to or not, he's going to marry us. *Today*.' Her smile made his heart flip.

'Tell me, Alex,' she said. 'Why *did* you hire another car? We could have come together, and we'd be married by now.'

He smiled. 'I wanted to see my bride walk down the aisle.'

Her mouth dropped open, surprise written on her face, her cheeks flushing with a tinge of pink. 'I had no idea you were such a romantic,' she whispered.

'There's a lot you don't know about me. But I'd like to change that,' he said. 'Now, give me your feet.'

She let him lift her feet onto his lap, turning on her seat to face him, her arm propped on the back of the seat, her head resting in her hands. He massaged her feet—they were dirty from walking barefoot. But he didn't care. She was here.

***

He was amazing.

Darcy had never once touched her feet—not to massage them or give her attention like this. But Alex? The way he moved his hands over her feet, not giving a damn about the cleanliness of them, the way he examined the swelling that had started on her ankle. The way he pressed his lips to her sore ankle, as though he was trying to kiss it better. It was intimate. It was nice. And it made her feel more for him than she ever had with anyone else.

He'd waited for her. She didn't know how long he'd been sitting in the hallway. But he was there, waiting for her to arrive, *knowing* she would come. And there they sat together, her feet in his lap, waiting for a chance to convince the celebrant to marry them. He'd come out to bring the next couple into the chapel room and glanced at them, shaking his head, and telling them he was booked out. She'd been convinced that was it. But Alex—he stayed put. Waiting, assuring her it was going to happen. Hours had passed, and couple after couple went into the room and came out happily married. And they sat— in silence, for the most part—waiting.

'I have a question,' Alex said, breaking their silence. She looked up at him with weary eyes, feeling the inside of her chest growing at the compassionate way he looked at her. 'Where's the photographer?'

Her eyes widened. Ciara had left just after her—she should have been here before her, but she hadn't even seen Ciara's car. If she *had,* she could have got a lift with her instead of walking.

'She never came?' she asked. Alex shook his head slowly. Great, so even the photographer bailed on them.

Alex tucked a curl behind her ear, refusing to break eye contact. 'So, it looks like everything that could go wrong, did,' he said, a hint of a smile across his lips. 'I don't get it Brigid. You're Irish, right? Aren't you supposed to be lucky?'

A laugh escaped her mouth—it wasn't graceful. More like a loud outburst that brought a flush of warmth to her cheeks. 'I don't think it works that way.'

'I think it should.' He rubbed his thumb across her cheek, and she felt the tingle of it shoot through her body down to her core.

She studied his eyes—so sincere, so tender. She swallowed the lump in her throat. 'Do you feel like everything's working against us?' she whispered. 'The car, my heels, the photographer, the celebrant. Do you think we're making a mistake?'

He pressed his palm to her cheek. She leaned into his hand, closing her eyes. She didn't want to believe they were making a mistake. She needed this marriage—so did he. But it wasn't just that. Brigid was starting to feel for this guy. Feelings she hadn't felt for anyone before and couldn't quite put a name to. Feelings that scared the hell out of her.

'I think it gives us more of a reason to fight for it.'

When she opened her eyes, he was leaning closer to her. She could feel her breath quickening and the warmth of his hand sliding to the back of her neck, his fingertips circling patterns on her skin. God, his touch. She nudged her lips closer to his, leaving only an inch between them—his eyes searching hers, and hers searching his—waiting for him to close the gap. She moved her hands up to cup his face, feeling the bristles of the whole three-day growth look he had going on. When they'd met, he'd been clean-shaven. But now, with the dark, soft bristles pressing against her palms, he was sexy as hell. She felt him move slowly to close the gap, but before their lips could touch, they heard a throat clear.

'I said I was booked out,' the celebrant said, his arms crossed over his chest.

'There's no one else here,' Alex stated calmly.

Brigid glanced at the clock on the wall. It was the end of the day, and Alex was right—there was no one else here.

'I'm closed.'

'Please?' Brigid said. 'We've been waiting for hours. It won't take long—you can even do the quick shortened version.'

'I said—'

'Name your price.' Alex stood, pulling his wallet from his pocket, and opening it up in front of the celebrant. 'Double?'

At first Brigid thought it might not work, but

when she saw the look on the celebrant's face when he saw all the notes in Alex's wallet, she was more worried he might try to rob them.

'Well, I'm supposed to be going home,' the celebrant said, his eyes green with greed. 'So, it really would be working overtime.'

Alex raised an eyebrow. 'Triple, then?' He pulled out a few notes, shoving them in the celebrant's hand. Brigid felt her eyes widen at the amount of money he'd just handed over with ease. How much did he *have*? 'Shall we?'

Alex took Brigid by the hand and pulled her to her feet, leading the way into the room and down to the end of the aisle, the celebrant not far behind them, stuffing the notes in his pocket. By the time they came to a stop at the end of the aisle and turned to face each other, Brigid couldn't tell if she was hyperventilating or if she'd stopped breathing altogether. Alex was looking at her with his striking green eyes wide with adventure. They were doing this. They were getting married.

***

Sure, the day hadn't gone exactly as planned. Everything he'd organised to make the day special for her had backfired. They should have been married by now, enjoying their first meal together as husband and wife, and headed home. Now, he imagined, they would be going through some kind of take-out joint—maybe even the same burger place as last night—before heading home. He wished they could have spent longer in Cork as a married couple, but the inn still had so much work to do and he'd stupidly booked for the windows to be delivered tomorrow.

They might feel like it was rushed. They might feel like it didn't go as they hoped. But it was still the best wedding he'd been to—it was his, with Brigid, and she was the most beautiful thing he'd ever seen. He could get lost in her eyes, his hands tangling in her hair, her lips on his. And he would enjoy every second of it. And he knew when he got that chance, it wouldn't be rushed.

The celebrant took his place beside them and cleared his throat. Alex glanced at him in time to see him eyeing Brigid's feet—her *bare* feet—with a look of disdain.

'Sorry,' Alex said.

He slipped his own shoes off and pulled his socks off, stuffing them in his shoes. He put them to the side and stood facing Brigid again. He could feel the celebrant's eyes boring into him, but he was focussed on the wild, amused eyes looking back at him.

'You two are the strangest couple I've had in here,' the celebrant muttered.

Alex didn't doubt it. The celebrant introduced the chapel witnesses and started reading off his script, but Alex didn't pay attention to anything other than the bride he was marrying, her eyes focussed on him, and her hands in his.

'Alex, do you take Brigid as your wife—for better, for worse, for richer, for poorer, in sickness and in health for as long as you both shall live?'

The celebrant's voice may have sounded flat, bored even. But the words rung in his ear as the promise they were.

'I do,' he said.

'Brigid, do you take Alex as your husband—for better, for worse, for richer, for poorer, in sickness and in health for as long as you both shall live?'

She didn't hesitate, her eyes flashing.

'I do.'

'Do you both promise to love and respect each other and care for each other, to remain faithful and be each other's best friend and supporter, and to raise your children together in unison?'

'We do.'

'Do you have rings?' the celebrant asked.

Brigid's eyes widened, and she looked as though she were about to say something when Alex responded. 'Yes.' She looked at him questioningly, her eyes glistening as he tugged the square box from his pocket, taking one of the rings—a thin gold band with an arrangement of tiny diamonds set into it, a small emerald in the centre—and passed the box to the celebrant.

'Go ahead,' the celebrant said.

He took Brigid's hand in his, placing the ring at the tip of her ring finger.

'Brigid, with this ring, I thee wed.'

He slid the ring onto her finger, relieved it was a

perfect fit. She blinked back tears, dabbing at her eyes with the back of her free hand before taking his wedding band from the box and placing it at the tip of his ring finger.

'Alex, with this ring, I thee wed.'

She slid the ring onto his finger and let out a shaky breath. He gave her a reassuring smile, even though he felt just as nervous as she looked. He took both of her hands in his and the celebrant wrapped a ribbon around their joined hands, forming the infinity symbol.

'What God has joined together, may no man separate. May He confirm your consent and this union and enrich you with His blessings.' The celebrant smiled for the first time during the ceremony as he unwrapped the ribbon, freeing their hands. 'I now pronounce you husband and wife. Alex, you may kiss your bride.'

Alex placed his hand at the back of her neck and met her halfway, his lips pressing against hers without any hesitation. He could feel the sparks flying between them, but what scared him most was that it felt like his lips belonged there—on hers—and she belonged there—in his arms. A smile tugged at his lips and he could feel her lips curving into a smile against his. He wondered if she had the same realisation he had—they had all the time in the world to discover what they had.

They were married.

It didn't take long for the celebrant to rush them through signing the certificate and push them out the door. But he didn't care, because by the end of the night, after finding somewhere for them to have a luxurious meal and packing up their things from the hotel room, he'd spent a lot of time with her hand in his, getting to know his *wife*. It was late by the time they got back to Kinsale, and they were both tired. But he grabbed their bags from the car and walked with Brigid up to her room. He placed her bag by the door and pulled her into his arms, holding her for a moment longer than he had held anyone before, and planted a kiss on the top of her head.

'Welcome home, Mrs Carter,' he whispered.

She looked up at him, her eyes dancing, and a smile on her face. 'Welcome home, Mr Carter.'

He brushed his lips against hers, softly, tenderly, and pulled away reluctantly, walking slowly towards his room. God, he hated that part of their arrangement. He'd love nothing more than to share the room with his wife, showing her the tenderness she deserved. Consummating a marriage was still a thing, right? But he'd promised to respect her. That included not doing anything against her wishes, even if it meant he wouldn't sleep at night. Because he sure as hell wouldn't be able to sleep knowing his wife was only a few rooms over.

'Alex?'

He turned at his name being called. Brigid was still standing by her door, her eyes on him, her hands twisting together in front of her. Her mouth opened and closed a few times as if she had something to say but decided against it. Finally, she spoke.

'Thank you.'

It wasn't what he'd hoped she was going to say, but he couldn't rush her. 'You're welcome,' he said, smiling. 'Goodnight, sweetheart.'

'Goodnight, Alex,' she said.

He watched as she entered her room and closed the door between them. He may have even still stayed looking at the closed door for a few minutes—he wasn't quite sure—before he found his feet again and went to his own room, a smile plastered on his face.

He was married.

To Brigid.

Chapter 14

'And here I thought he couldn't be tamed.'

'Who?'

'Alex got married.'

'*What*?'

Alex watched the exchange happening on the screen in front of him. After a day like yesterday, he'd figured it was probably time to tell his best friend he was married—two weeks after his own wedding. Olivia nudged Scott to the side, coming into view.

'Are you serious, Alex?' she said. 'When?'

'Yesterday,' he said, trying his best to contain his laugh at Olivia's enthusiasm. 'I know, it's a bit surprising, but it's what works best for us.'

'Wow,' Olivia said. 'Well, I'm really happy for you

both. You know, I was wondering why she called me wondering where you were, but … wow. I'm going to kill her for not telling me.'

Alex squinted. She called Olivia? How the hell— 'Brigid called you?'

'What? Brigid? No, Betty called me. Who's Brigid?'

'My *wife*.'

Olivia's eyes widened. 'Oh, you weren't talking about … you know, I think my phone's ringing. I better … congratulations, Alex. I really am happy for you.'

Olivia left the screen quicker than she'd appeared on it. Scott was looking in the direction she went, then turned his attention back to Alex, his eyebrow raised. 'That's some big news, mate.'

'I need you to tell me your secrets to a good marriage.'

Scott laughed. 'I've been married two weeks, Alex,' he said. 'But I'll tell you what it is—she's always right. *Always*.'

'What was she saying about Betty?' he asked, hesitantly.

Scott grimaced. 'Trust me—you don't want to know.'

Know what? Why would Betty be wondering where he was? Unless she wanted to patch things up between them. But, surely not. She should know him well enough to know he only ever gave out one chance. One chance and that's it—if you blow it, you don't get another. Besides, she'd left him for another man. Why the hell would she be interested in what he's doing?

'Wha—bu—sh—'

And why the hell couldn't he wrap his head around the very thought of it? Scott moved closer to the screen.

'Alex, forget her.' His voice was firm. 'She screwed you over. She's history. But now, you're with Brigid—you're *married* to Brigid, which I'm still amazed at, by the way, since you've only been there for two weeks. And whatever happened for you guys to fall in love so quickly, remember that. That's real.'

Alex tilted his head, squinting. 'Well …'

Scott dropped his head backwards. 'Alex!' He drew his name out with a mixture of exhaustion and exasperation. 'What the hell did you do?'

'We made an agreement,' he said, shrugging. 'We both needed something and getting married sorted that out. It was … convenient.'

'*Convenient*?' Scott repeated. Alex was glad they were talking over the internet instead of face to face. He was sure Scott would have him pinned to the ground trying to talk some sense into him. 'You got married because it was *convenient*?'

'Well, not entirely,' he said. 'I mean, it started out like that, but then we started to get to know each other. It's … more … now.'

Scott smiled, shaking his head. 'You son of a bitch,' he teased. 'You *are* in love with her!'

'No, I'm not!' he said. 'I mean, maybe. I don't know. I guess we're … getting there.' Was he?

'Ugh, I'm going to go before this gets too mushy.'

'Like you're one to talk! I had to put up with your mushiness over Olivia, remember?'

'Whatever, dude,' Scott said. 'Look, I'm glad you found someone to get there with. She must be a nice girl to make you start thinking about any kind of marriage.'

'Thanks, asshole.'

'Now, if you'll excuse me, I've got to go get there with *my* wife.'

Scott winked at the screen and Alex rolled his eyes. Like he needed that visual. He pushed the screen of his laptop down and went downstairs. He'd contemplated checking on Brigid to see if she was awake yet, but he'd decided she needed the rest—especially if she was freaking out like he was. How was he supposed to feel the day after getting married? Maybe in a normal marriage it would be a bit different. But now, it was as though nothing changed, yet the whole world was different. He had a wife. But they hadn't done any of the normal couple rituals to prove it. What was the common curtesy in this situation? Should he wake her up with a kiss even though she was staying in a separate room, or should he just carry on as usual?

With his hand raised to knock on her door and a battle raging inside of him as to what he should do, he was relieved to hear a truck pulling up outside the inn, making the decision for him. He'd organised the windows to be delivered, and they were here. It was a matter that had to be tended to. Even if he felt like he was leaving his heart in the room where his sleeping wife lay.

***

'So nice of you to join us,' Alex teased as Lee met them for the next window pane.

Alex and Ailbe had been unloading the windows from the truck and taking them to their respective locations for the past twenty minutes. Lee was supposed to be at the inn before the truck but, for some reason, was late, which was apparently out of the ordinary for him if Ailbe's reaction was anything to go off.

'Everythin' all right, lad?' he said, his brow furrowed.

Lee scratched the stubble on his chin—he obviously hadn't had a chance to shave, either. He nodded, looking over at Alex. 'You know, Moira wasn't very happy to hear her best friend got married without telling her.'

'Brigid didn't tell her?'

Tell her what? That she was going to get married but she wasn't invited? Would she have wanted Moira to be her maid of honour? Colleen to be her bridesmaid and her daddy to walk her down the aisle? Or Aislinn to be her flower girl? God, Brigid would know at least half the town! Surely, she would have wanted all of her friends and family there at her wedding. And he'd taken that from her—hadn't even given her the option to have anyone she cared about there. Was it because he had no one to bring? Had he just selfishly assumed that, given the situation, she didn't want anyone to witness it?

They could have been married in Kinsale if she wanted. He only organised it in Cork because he'd figured it had to be kept on the down low. But had she even told her daddy and her sister that they went to Cork to get married? Had she been too ashamed of him to make the commitment in front of her friends and family?

'Apparently not.' Lee shrugged, helping Alex lift a window from the truck. 'So, of course, I had to calm her down. Then, she got straight on to planning.'

'Planning?' Alex asked. He heard Ailbe snicker as he passed by to clear a space for the window he and Lee carried.

Lee's lips curved into a sly grin. 'The party—for you and Brigid. A reception party, of sorts. She figured she'd plan it since you weren't able to share your *special day* with friends and family.'

Alex exhaled. A party. To celebrate their marriage. He'd been prepared that the people she was close to might not approve of their decision. But throwing them a party? He hadn't expected that. Threats to hurt him if he hurt her, sure. But he hadn't expected any kind of celebration. After all, everyone he'd met knew they'd only known each other for two weeks. He was surprised her daddy even bought the story that they'd met before. He shuddered. *Her daddy*. Alex had worked hard to get his semi-approval. Was marrying his daughter without involving him in any part of it digging his own shallow grave?

'She shouldn't have gone to the trouble,' he said. 'I mean, she's busy enough as is. But thank you, I mean it. Would … would Brigid be okay with it though? Is she a party person?'

They leaned the window against the wall that Ailbe cleared. Lee shrugged. 'She's your wife, shouldn't you know that?' he teased. 'But seriously, we were hoping you'd be able to convince her.'

Alex sighed. Thing is, *he* wasn't much of a party person, despite what people might have thought about him in the past. But Brigid needed this. Whether reality had already hit her or not, they were married. There was no getting around it. Brigid had to celebrate this milestone with the people she cared about.

'All right,' he said. 'I'll try. When's the party?'

'Tonight, Mr Carter,' Ailbe said, slapping Alex on the back.

'Wait, how did you know?' Lee asked, his brow furrowed.

'Yer lovely lass called me as soon as ye were out the door, I reckon,' Ailbe said, his belly laugh vibrating through Alex's eardrums. 'And I know Moira. She's a real last-minute planner.'

Lee shook his head slowly. 'She said I'd forget, you know,' he said. 'But I didn't, did I? Make sure you tell her Al.'

All right. So, he had a party to get to tonight. A party he needed to convince Brigid to go to. And hopefully, to act as an icebreaker to any post-wedding awkwardness they might have.

'Oh, and one more thing,' Lee said hesitantly. 'Moira wasn't sure if Brigid's daddy and Colleen knew you two tied the knot. She hasn't invited them just in case, hoping you and Brigid could pass on the details for her.'

Alex nodded. 'I'll ask her.'

***

Brigid tucked her hair into the messy bun, letting her fingertips linger where she could still feel Alex's touch. She squinted in the mirror. Was she supposed to feel different? Did being married have a different feel to it than being single that she was missing out on? She studied the ring on her finger—so elegant, so pretty, so *her*. It felt natural on her finger, like it had sat there for a long time, even though it had been less than a day. She rubbed at her tired eyes.

Maybe she didn't feel any different because nothing really was different. Sure, legally, she was married—Mrs Brigid Carter. But how had their relationship changed? They still knew barely anything about each other and they'd done nothing more than a kiss. But they were married. They'd promised the rest of their lives to each other despite all of that. Despite the fact that they never got along to begin with. Despite their histories, knowing what their future was going to hold—the inn, a child who wasn't his, and maybe, one day, some that were.

Despite the feelings that were growing, making her feel like a fool. But she shouldn't feel like a fool, right? It was normal for a woman to have feelings for her husband.

It's just that nothing was normal about their relationship.

She'd been so close to asking him to come into her room with her last night. So close to asking for more. But she freaked out. She was scared to ask her husband to spend the night with her, even though she'd wanted it more than anything she'd ever wanted in her life. He made her feel things she'd never felt before. He'd put her in uncharted territory. She'd put it down to the excitement of their day—they had just got hitched, after all. All the romance, the chemistry, the natural high they'd been on for doing something crazy. She'd wondered if she still would have felt like she wanted him so much when she woke up in the morning.

She did.

Maybe more so since she couldn't sleep all night with her mind on two things—him. And what he would feel like laying on top of her. She'd imagined he was different to Darcy. Darcy had been inattentive and selfish. As though sex was designed for men and men only to enjoy. He had no mindfulness of her. Alex would be different—she was sure of it. He was a totally different man to Darcy. Already, he'd shown thoughtfulness and showed he cared for her, which was more than Darcy had ever done. She'd imagined Alex had a tender touch—the kind that could get you almost to the tipping point. She'd imagined it would be romantic, magical. And while her mind was raging with thoughts of the man sleeping a few rooms down the hall from her, sleep was impossible. She'd even considered going to his room but didn't want to appear desperate.

She pressed her hand to her stomach. Would they have ever married if it wasn't for her being pregnant? Sure, Alex needed to get citizenship to keep the inn. But he could have asked any girl and they would have agreed in a heartbeat. She'd seen the way girls swooned over him. Would he have asked her? And would she have agreed if there was nothing really in it for her? Maybe she would have still been hung up on being Darcy's mistress. A knock on the door startled her from her thoughts.

'Come in,' she said, realising she probably shouldn't have been so quick to invite whoever was on the other side of the door into her room. She sighed in relief when Alex poked his head through the door.

'Is it safe?' he asked.

He didn't wait for a reply before stepping into the room. Brigid was still standing near her mirror, her cheeks flushed from having the very object of her fantasies appearing at the same time she'd been thinking of him. She'd hoped he was going to sweep her into his arms—at least give her a kiss. But he didn't. He remained near the door, leaving it ajar. Had the thought not even crossed his mind? She folded her arms over her chest, feeling the stupid need to hide her body, despite being fully dressed.

His mouth opened and closed, as though he was going to say something but thought better of it. His eyes studied her. His gorgeous, green eyes that were softened today, looking at her with something she hadn't seen before in his expression.

'Hey,' he said, his voice smooth.

'Hi,' she said, shakily.

'I, umm ... did you sleep well?'

He glanced towards her bed before looking back at her. He was leaning against the wall next to the door, his hands in his pockets. Was she imagining the awkwardness between them? She flashed him the best smile she could muster which, she had to admit, was pretty pathetic, and shrugged.

'It could have been better,' she admitted.

She thought she saw his shoulders drop slightly. 'Oh,' he said. Did he sound disappointed? 'I hope you weren't ... regretting ... us.'

Regret? Her mind caught up and she realised why he'd sounded disappointed. 'Oh, no,' she said, taking an awkward step towards him. 'It's not that. I think I was just still on a high from the ... events ... of yesterday, that's all. My mind was racing all night, so it took a while for me to fall asleep.' Which wasn't a lie—her mind *was* racing all night, just from something a little different to what she was implying.

'So, no regrets?' he said, standing up a little straighter, his eyebrow raised.

She shook her head, a more sincere smile on her

face. 'None.' Unless wishing she'd invited him to stay with her counted as a regret.

His lips curved into a toothy grin. God, he was gorgeous. If just his smile could send her stomach flipping like this, she'd be putty in his hands if they did anything more. The very thought of it sent a shiver down her spine.

'Good,' he said, his smooth voice reverberating through her. 'So, I need to talk to you about something, and I'm not sure how you'll react.'

She furrowed her brow. 'What is it?'

'Did ... did you want anyone to be at the wedding?'

She felt her heart drop in her chest. 'I hadn't really thought about it,' she said, slowly. Should she have? Wasn't a girl supposed to dream of getting married with all of her family and friends around? The thought hadn't even crossed her mind. 'I guess it just happened so quickly.'

He bit his lower lip and dropped his gaze to the floor for a moment. When he looked back at her, there was a deepness in his eyes. Sincerity. Apology. 'I'm sorry, if you'd wanted anyone else there,' he said. 'I don't know why I didn't think of it before.'

She barely felt her feet close the distance between them, or her hands touching his arms. 'Alex, no, you thought of everything. It was incredible.'

'I didn't think of *that*, Brigid,' he said. His voice was firm, but a little shaky. It put her at a loss for words. 'A wedding is supposed to be the best day of your life and I didn't—' He pinched the bridge of his nose and closed his eyes. 'I know it wasn't exactly a conventional wedding and it was rushed, but I didn't think you might have wanted to have your friends and family there. I should have thought of that.'

She cupped her hand against his cheek. 'It wouldn't have been fair on you, Alex,' she said, smoothing her thumb over his cheek. He held her gaze—it was captivating. 'You didn't have anyone to bring, it would have been unfair if I'd brought everyone I know.' She dropped her hand to hold his. 'Besides, I like it better this way. We got to share something special with each other, no one else spectating or judging. Just us.'

His eyes studied her. She was sure he could see right into the depths of her soul and see the butterflies batting against the walls of her stomach. He squeezed her hand.

'Promise?' he said.

'Promise.'

'So, it's not because you were embarrassed to be marrying me?'

His words caught her off guard. Embarrassed? She was embarrassed she'd been fooled by Darcy. Embarrassed she'd been put in a situation where she had to get married to save face. She was embarrassed of Darcy. But she'd managed to marry the new stud in town which, she was sure, a lot of ladies would be jealous of. But not only was he sexy as hell, he was a gentleman who had treated her with respect and cared for her in more ways than could be expected of someone you've just met. She took a shaky breath.

'I could never be embarrassed of you, Alex,' she whispered.

His eyes were focussed on her as though checking the sincerity of her words. Then, that mischievous look she was growing fond of flashed across his face.

'Are you sure about that?' he asked. She squinted, looking at him questioningly. He tugged her closer, wrapping his arms around her waist. 'Because I'm sure I could think of ways to be embarrassing.'

'It wasn't a challenge, Mr Carter,' she warned, pressing her hands against his chest. God, he smelled good.

'Mmm, it sounded like a challenge to me,' he said. 'You should know not to tempt me, Mrs Carter.'

'Is that so?' His lips were only inches from hers.

'Mhmm,' he hummed. 'But we'll have to explore that another time because, my dear, we have a party to attend tonight.'

She pushed back. 'A party? What for?'

'For you,' he said. 'And me. To celebrate.'

'You planned a *party*?'

'Not me,' he said. 'Moira has, since we didn't have anyone come to the wedding.'

Oh, God. Her daddy and Colleen—she was on her way to tell them they'd got married. Had Moira beaten her to it? She could feel the beads of sweat forming on her forehead as she imagined what their faces would look like when she met up with them. Would they be happy for her? Would they be annoyed they'd heard it from someone else? God, she was sure they were already going to be hurt to find out she hadn't told them when she was getting married. Truth is, she didn't want it to be a big event. She didn't want to be judged or criticised or anything. Most of all, she didn't want Darcy to know where they were getting married, which would have been guaranteed if she'd invited anyone.

Most girls would have been dreaming about their wedding since they were a child. Brigid was not one of those girls. To her, a wedding was just a formality. Sure, she'd figured her daddy would have walked her down the aisle, and Colleen and Moira would have been her bridesmaids, but she'd always hoped it would be simple, elegant, and not crowded. Then again, she couldn't have imagined a more perfect wedding than the one she'd just had—even with everything going wrong.

'You haven't told your daddy and Colleen yet, have you?' he asked, his eyebrow raised.

'I was just on my way to,' she mumbled. 'But if Moira—'

'She hasn't told them.'

She felt a wave of relief wash over her. 'She hasn't?'

Alex shook his head slowly. 'She wasn't sure if you'd told them or not, so she thought she'd leave inviting them up to you.'

'That was ... very thoughtful of her.'

Brigid studied one of her fingernails that was starting to split and realised she still had her hands pressed against his chest. Reluctantly, she dropped her hands and took a step back. She felt his hands drop from her hips and the disappointment that came with it.

'So, you're okay with the party? You don't want me to cancel it—have a quiet night in?' He had that mischievous look in his eyes and his lips pulled to one side.

'No, we should have it,' she said, wondering what a quiet night in with Alex would be like. 'Moira's probably already invited the town and has it all planned.'

'Then, in that case, you should go see your daddy.' He squeezed her hand and brushed a quick kiss against her cheek. 'Are you sure you don't want me to come with you?'

She shook her head, feeling the warmth of his lips lingering on the spot he kissed. She wished he could be there, holding her hand, being her support while she broke the news to her daddy and Colleen that they'd eloped. But he couldn't. She didn't know how they were going to react to the news. She could take whatever was thrown her way. But Alex had already been given the third-degree from her daddy. She didn't want him being subjected to more.

'I need to do this.'

Chapter 15

'So, from all of us here, I'd like to say big
congratulations to the happy couple,' Lee said, lifting
his glass. 'When it's true love, there's no point in
waiting, right?'

Lee slapped Alex on the back and Brigid let out an
awkward chuckle. If only Lee knew the half of it. Or
maybe he did—maybe he just had the common
courtesy to keep their situation private. She stared
into her glass of sparkling apple juice, disappointed
she couldn't have anything stronger. She blinked
back the tears that were threatening to spill as she
thought about her lunch with Colleen and their
daddy. She'd expected them to be surprised. She'd
expected them to take a few moments to process
the news. She'd wasted no time beating around the

bush—spilling the news before they'd even had a chance to order. Why bother making light, awkward conversation when she was about to drop a bombshell on them?

She hadn't expected the silence. She hadn't expected her daddy's slumped shoulders as he processed the news. She hadn't expected him to stand up and tell Colleen they were leaving without saying anything to Brigid. Or the hurt in Colleen's eyes as she silently obeyed. She'd followed them to their car, begging her daddy to hear her out. She'd stopped his car door from closing with her hand.

'Daddy, please,' she'd said, tears in her eyes. 'This is what I wanted. I wanted to have a simple wedding, just me and Alex. I didn't want to wait for a big wedding to be planned. I'm sorry I hurt you, but this is what *I* wanted.'

He'd only stared ahead, but Colleen was looking at her, her eyes glistening. She couldn't have them thinking it was Alex's idea—even if it was—or tell him the real reason why they'd gotten married so quickly. She couldn't give him any kind of ammunition to use against Alex, because the truth was she'd wanted—needed—this as much as Alex did. It may have started out as an arrangement, but she was certain she had genuine feelings for him and they would, with time, fall in love. Colleen had opened her mouth as if about to say something and closed it after looking at their daddy. Brigid understood. Colleen couldn't afford to get on their daddy's bad side, not when he was this upset with

Brigid.

'Moira's throwing a party for us tonight at their place,' she continued. 'And it would mean a lot to me if you were both there.'

He continued staring ahead, Brigid's heart pounding and the ache spreading through her chest. She hadn't bothered holding the tears back. Colleen and her daddy were the only family she had. Sure, Ailbe, Lee, and Moira were like family to her. But Colleen and her daddy were blood. Blood isn't supposed to exile you or shut you out for making a decision. But sometimes, they're the ones who do.

'Daddy?' she'd said, the tears choking her.

'Remove your hand, Brigid.' His tone was cold and sent a chill washing through her.

'But ... Colleen?'

'I—' Colleen started but got cut off by their daddy's hand sliding up between them, and he looked at her for the first time since she'd shared the news.

'*You* chose to shut us out, Brigid. Remove. Your. Hand.'

His stern voice and the lack of any kind of emotion in his eyes shattered her like a china vase crashing against the ground. She'd released the door and watched as they drove away—not another word, not another glance—her blood, doing exactly what she'd tried to avoid.

Brigid blinked away the haze the memory had created and swiped at the tears that had filled her eyes. She wasn't going to cry—not at the party her true family was throwing for her and Alex. Why couldn't her daddy have been supportive of them? And what of Colleen? Would they act like they didn't know her if she saw them in the street? Had she lost all ties with the two people she had cared most for in the world? She felt the warmth of Alex's arms wrapping around her, his body against her back, and she realised how it felt to be protected. Alex was her family now. They were married. And she had no doubt he wouldn't turn his back on her.

'Everything all right?' he whispered into her ear.

She rubbed her thumb against his interlocked arms and nodded. 'I just hoped they would come,' she mumbled, pressing back against him. God, he felt so warm, so right, their bodies perfectly fit together.

'I'm sorry,' he said, his voice soothing, warm—a vast contrast to what her daddy's was at lunch that day. He pressed his soft lips just below her ear, sending a tingle through her body. 'But you still have all these people who love you and support you—they support us.'

She closed her eyes and enjoyed his warmth. He was right. There were certainly more people at the party than she'd thought there would be. And each and every one of them seemed genuinely happy for her and Alex. She breathed in his scent—a smell she was becoming accustomed to that made her crave more of him. She hoped he felt the same about her as she did of him. He'd promised her fidelity, support, even love. And he'd done everything he could to surprise her with sweet sentiments on their wedding day. And his touches since then.

Even if his affection at the party was for show, she knew their embrace in her room was not. And now, more than ever, she wanted him. She wanted all of him. She wanted to feel his kisses caressing her body, his skin on hers. She wanted to take him in and get lost with him. And maybe, if she could find some way to actually enjoy the party, tonight would be that night. They *were* married, after all.

'I'll leave you to it,' he said, squeezing her briefly.

She felt the cool breeze against her back as he pulled away and she reluctantly opened her eyes, feeling her breath stop as she saw her sister standing only a few feet away from her. *She came*. Colleen stepped closer and pulled Brigid into a hug.

'God, Brigid, I'm so sorry,' she muttered. 'I'm happy for you, I am. I mean, sure, I was disappointed I wasn't there, but I understand why you had to do it. Daddy's just ... well ... he's an ass.'

'Is he—'

Colleen shook her head before Brigid could finish. 'He wouldn't come,' she said. 'He wouldn't listen to reason, either. As soon as we got home, he shut himself in his study.'

'Is he all right?' Sure, she may be upset he'd reacted like that, and mad at him for it. But he was still her daddy.

Colleen shrugged, exhausted. 'My bets are he's still sitting at his desk, glass in his hand, staring at the bottle of whisky. Ironically, the same bottle Alex gave him.'

Brigid forced out a chuckle. Ironic, indeed. She scanned the crowd around them, her eyes stopping at the clearing in the hedge where the front gate was. It was dark in that corner, but she could make out a shadow that shouldn't be there. A shadow that was shaped uncannily familiar. She felt the cold breeze pick up, a shiver racking her body as she felt her blood drain to her toes. Colleen tugged at her sleeve.

'Brigid? Are you all right?' She glanced at her sister, concern spread on her face. 'You look as though you've seen a ghost.'

She tried to speak, but the words didn't come. Another gust of wind swept through the yard and she glanced to the dark corner again. The shadow was gone. But she'd seen it.

She'd seen *him*.

***

Brigid's mood had improved after her sister came to the party, but Alex couldn't help but notice something seemed to be bothering her. He figured it was the fact that her daddy—the arrogant bastard—hadn't bothered to show any kind of support for their marriage, or even show up to their party. He couldn't even imagine why anyone would turn their back on their child like Mr Murphy did. He certainly wouldn't turn his back on any of his children—even the one Brigid carried now. As far as he was concerned, that child was his. He or she would grow up knowing him as their father, and no one would be any the wiser. But for now, it was one step at a time.

'Thanks, again, for the party,' he said, shaking Lee's hand, and giving Moira a hug.

He wrapped his arm around Brigid to keep her warm from the cold breeze as they said their final goodbyes for the evening. They'd stayed until the last of the guests had left and helped Lee and Moira clean up. Now, it was late, and he was tired—they both were. He could see it in Brigid's drooping eyes. But he also felt the warmth expanding his chest as he caught a glimpse of Brigid's smile.

They'd walked to the party since the inn wasn't far away. And now, they walked back, his arm around her shoulders, nothing but the still of the night and the breeze rustling in the trees disturbing them. She was glowing, but he could still see a hint of worry in her expression. On the other hand, nothing felt as perfect as having his arm draped around her, feeling her body move against his as they walked side by side. Though, he could think of something that might be better...

'Thank you, Alex,' Brigid said, her voice quiet, her eyes sincere as she looked up at him. The glint in her eyes made his breath catch. 'For everything. I don't know where I'd be right now if it wasn't for you.'

She'd probably still have a relationship with her daddy, for starters. He had no doubt Brigid would have worked something out. She was the kind of girl who could always land on her feet—he was sure of it. It was one of the things he found attractive about her. Her independence, her stubbornness. The glimpses he catches in her eyes of something more—something unexplainable. But if he had to give it a go, he'd say she was letting him in. And while it scared the hell out of him, it also excited him in more ways than one.

He'd never moved as fast with anyone as he did with Brigid. Of course, she trumped any girlfriends he'd had, since they were already married now. He hadn't even considered marriage with anyone else, which is probably why his proposition to Brigid surprised him more than it may have surprised her. The fact a woman as strong and beautiful as her agreed to marry him had him at a loss for words.

He was certain she could have had any man she'd wanted, so why him? He'd seen the way the men looked at her as they passed by, and he'd be lying if he said it didn't make him jealous. He wanted to give her everything. He wanted to give her all of him, and to have all of her. He wanted to feel things for her—with her—and he was certain he was already there. He wouldn't go so far as saying he loved her yet, but he knew that time was getting closer very quickly. He just hoped she felt the same.

Would she have agreed to be with him if she wasn't in the predicament she was in? Not many women would be up for marrying to help a man gain citizenship if there wasn't anything in it for them. But even if he didn't need to gain citizenship—if they'd met and neither of them had anything a marriage of convenience would fix. If they were just a man and a woman, two souls crossing paths, would she have chosen him? He knew what his answer would be. Brigid was breathtakingly beautiful—there was no denying it—and from the second he saw her, he'd wanted her. But would she have wanted him?

'What do you mean?' Brigid's voice jarred him out of his thoughts, her tone laced with warmth and a bit of confusion—possibly as much confusion as he felt.

'Hmm?' Alex opened the door of the inn for Brigid and followed her inside. He must have been so focussed on his thoughts that he'd blanked on most of the walk home—and apparently talked.

'Well, you didn't say anything all the way home and then you asked if I would have wanted you,' she explained.

Shoot. He felt his cheeks warm but brushed the feeling aside. He couldn't have her thinking he hadn't meant to ask her something his subconscious went ahead and did for him. They started up the stairs, Alex unable to take his eyes off her ass as it swayed in front of him.

'If neither of us were in this situation, would you have wanted me?'

She stopped mid-step and turned to face him. She was a couple of steps higher than him, so he took another step until their bodies were almost touching. It brought his eyes level with hers—God, they were enchanting.

'Would you even be here if we weren't?' she asked, resting her hands on his shoulders, her slender fingers circling the base of his neck. He furrowed his brow. 'I mean, you wouldn't be here if it wasn't for the inn. You could have sold it to the highest bidder—some developer, or something—but you didn't. You'd already decided you'd keep the inn. And that meant you needed citizenship.'

'Would you have wanted me if you weren't pregnant?'

His voice was a little over a whisper, but he knew she could hear. He slid his hands around her waist, holding onto her. He didn't know why his breath caught in his chest as though he was waiting in anticipation for what her answer was—as though everything depended on what she said. Maybe it was just his ego. Or maybe his next move did depend on it. His eyes searched hers, looking for anything—*anything*—that could soothe the unexplainable ache in his chest and the heaviness in his stomach. Her supple lips curved into a sly smile, her tongue darting out to moisten her lower lip before she bit into it.

'What makes you so sure I wanted you as it was?' she said.

He knew she was teasing, but it made a large part of him throb with desire and the blood drain from his head. He kissed goodbye to any rational thought for however long it took for Brigid to have her fill of him. He was entirely at her disposal, and the very thought of being close to her, their bodies moving against each other, aroused him more than he already was.

'Because I wanted you,' he said, his voice more of a growl than anything. 'Because I *want* you.'

Her lips parted, and he could feel the small breath of air puff out between them, her smell awakening something inside him—something untamed, unrelenting. He felt the rumble at the base of his throat as she dug her fingertips into his shoulders, and he knew he was gone. Her breaths were quickening—sharp and shallow—and she looked as though there was a battle of words going through her mind, each fighting to make its way out her lips. It was barely a whisper, but he heard it loud and clear.

'I want you.'

***

She was lost in his eyes. She saw the slight delay as he processed her words, and she'd hoped he wouldn't think better of it. It was true—she wanted him. More now than ever, with his closeness, and his touch, and his smell. God, she wanted him. The chemistry between them caused a heady tension she couldn't explain, couldn't deny. She could only say that the pulsing through her body and the yearning she had for him from somewhere so deep inside she didn't know existed had made her lose any resolve. His brief hesitation felt like hours when it was probably no more than a couple of seconds, and then, his lips were on hers.

The same lips she'd dreamed of in the few moments she'd managed to get any sleep. The same lips that left the lingering addictive taste of him for days. The very lips she'd hoped wouldn't stop kissing her, taking her into an oblivion of bliss for the rest of their lives. His tongue darted between her parted lips, searching her mouth, and teasing her every sensation. Addictive was an understatement.

She wrapped her arms around the back of his neck, pressing her body against his. He wasted no time, dropping his hands from her waist to her thighs and lifting her with ease, his lips refusing to leave hers, and took the last of the stairs effortlessly, bringing them to the door of her room. Her legs were wrapped around him and she could feel his body tense beneath his clothes as though he was fighting the primal urge to take her where they stood. The very thought made her body pulse with anticipation and wanting. She laced her fingers through his hair, letting a gasp escape as he moved his lips from hers across her chin and down her neck.

'Keys,' he mumbled against the side of her neck.

The headiness of his kisses banished any form of logical thought. 'Hmm?'

'*Keys*,' he repeated, his voice rumbling against her neck and sending a vibration shooting through the rest of her body.

God, if he would just stop kissing her for a second to let her mind work out what he was trying to say. But she didn't want him to stop. Ever. She wanted him to make her his, to lay claim on every inch of her, emotionally, and physically. Especially physically.

'Where are your damn keys?'

'Oh, God,' she gasped as his teeth caught a bit of

skin on her neck. Why weren't they already in her room making sweet, sweet love and getting downright dirty on any surface they could make it to?

'Brigid,' he breathed, nipping and sucking at the sensitive spot of her neck.

'Mmm.' It felt so good, so right, feeling his touch, his kisses, hearing her name on his lips. Wait, what was it he was asking? Keys, right. 'Oh, umm ... back pocket ... I think.' She wasn't entirely sure.

He pressed her against the door, pinning her in place to free one of his hands, smoothing it up her thigh and into the back pocket of her jeans. He squeezed her ass and moved his hand back to it's original spot on her thigh, repeating the sequence with his other hand, but pulling her keys from the pocket on its return. Bringing his lips back to hers, he kept kissing her, searching her mouth. She met his kisses with the same vigour he had and in a flurry of jingling keys and passion, he was laying her down on her bed. She started fumbling at the buttons of his shirt as he tugged hers over her head, breaking the kisses only to let the fabric pass between them. He moved his lips down her neck again, leaving a trail of kisses across her clavicle and over the mounds of her breasts. She finally got the damn buttons undone in time to press her hands against his bare chest as he slid his underneath her singlet.

'I've got ... protection ... in my room,' he muttered between kisses. 'I'll go get it.'

He pulled away, but she grabbed hold of his

hand. 'No,' she whispered. 'I don't want to wait any longer.' His brow creased, and she ran her thumb across the line. She flashed him a smile. 'It's not like I'll get pregnant,' she added. 'I want to feel you. All of you.'

He leaned close and pressed his lips tenderly against hers. She could feel him holding back, but she didn't want him to. She didn't just want him—she needed him. He squeezed her hand and pulled back enough to rest his forehead against hers.

'At least let me get your present from the car,' he said, his eyes pleading. 'I was going to wait, but I want to give it to you now.'

She pouted her lips, even though curiosity got the better of her. 'Can't it wait until after?'

His smile sent another pulse through her body and she couldn't shake the feeling of disappointment as he brushed a kiss across her forehead and pulled away. 'Patience, sweetheart.'

She watched as the door swung closed behind him and jumped to her feet. She hadn't wanted him to leave for any amount of time, not with where they were headed, but at least the few moments would give her time to freshen up. She splashed some water on her face and brushed her teeth. In the renovations, Alex had been careful to make sure she had a fresh bathroom to go with her room. Most of the rooms had their own bathroom anyway, but he'd really gone all out. She grabbed her brush and ran it through her hair, tying it into a bun then letting it out. Was Alex the kind of man who liked to run his fingers through her hair while they made love?

She heard the door open and close quietly and the lock click behind it. She smiled. That wasn't enough time for him to go to the car and be back— he would have barely made it out of the inn. Maybe he decided the present could wait, after all. Just as well—she was sure she was going to go insane if he'd taken a moment longer. She adjusted her shirt so she showed more cleavage than she usually would and left the bathroom, stopping in her tracks to see him standing there, a cold chill racing down her spine from the crazy look in his eyes that was what nightmares were made of and a snarl that bared his teeth like a wolf.

'Hello, Brigid.'

She slid along the wall towards the lamp—the closest thing she could use as a weapon. 'Get out,' she said, her voice shaky despite all her efforts.

She glanced to where the lamp should be, but it was gone. Scanning the room sent her heart dropping to her stomach. Anything she could have used to defend herself had been removed. But how? Or rather, when? Had the room already been swept clean before her and Alex had come in? She hadn't noticed. She'd only been focussed on Alex and his kisses. And no doubt, that's all he'd been focussed on too.

He shook his head, his tongue clicking, and moved towards her. She caught a glimpse of something shiny and silver in his right hand held against his leg. Was that a...

'I gave you time, Brigid,' he said, each step making her insides shudder. She kept sliding against the wall, trying to keep the distance between them, but he'd had her cornered. 'I warned you, and you didn't listen.'

'You were there,' she whispered. 'It *was* you. At the party. Wasn't it?'

'Damn right it was,' he said, a wicked laugh escaping. 'Do you really think marrying that ponce would save you?'

He jerked his arm against her chest, pinning her against the wall, and she saw it—a knife—as he swayed it between them. God, this was it. He was going to kill her the day after she married someone she could truly love. She fought against him, but he was too strong, and she could smell the stench of alcohol on his breath.

'You don't have to do this,' she pleaded. 'You're off the hook, Darcy. No one will know. Everyone will believe the baby is his.'

He pressed harder, making it more difficult for her to breathe, and brought his face close to hers. 'No bastard will call my child his!' he growled.

She felt the cool of the knife press against her stomach and for the first time in her life, she felt truly afraid. Not of dying. Not of pain. But afraid of missing out on something that could have been genuine, beautiful, with a man who cared about her—the man who was the type of man she'd never believed existed until she met him. She felt Darcy's body shaking as he pushed against her and sucked her stomach in—a feeble attempt to get away from the knife.

'You should have listened, Brigid,' he continued. 'Instead, you paraded around with that guy acting like you're in love with him. Well, you didn't fool me, Brigid. I know the truth.'

She felt her blood boiling, her shallow breaths quickening. If he was going to kill her, she wasn't going to let him have the satisfaction of thinking he'd won.

'I'm more in love with him than I ever was with you,' she spat. His eyes widened and raged with fury, but she wasn't going to stop. 'You disgust me.'

She gasped a raspy breath as he forced the knife into her stomach. She heard a cry around them, a high-pitched, blood-curdling scream, as he forced it in again and pulled it out. It took a moment for her to realise it was her who made the noise. Her legs gave way and she slid down the wall, her hand clutching her stomach, her face wet. Darcy grasped her chin in his hand and leaned down towards her, forcing her to look at him, even though she was losing consciousness.

'I warned you,' he snarled. 'You should have listened.'

The malicious look on Darcy's face might be the last thing she ever saw, but Alex was all she could think of. His touch, his smell. Everything about him she would never have again.

Alex.

Chapter 16

Alex practically ran towards his car, a skip in his step, the cold brisk air refreshing, his heart pounding in his chest. It was going to happen. Brigid wanted him. And he wanted her—more than anything. And he was moments away from having her—all of her. He could have waited to give her the necklace he'd bought her. But he needed an excuse to get some fresh air. He wanted things to last with Brigid. He wanted their first time to be special. He wanted to take his time learning her body and giving her the attention she deserved. And he was worried if he didn't take a breather, it would be over quicker than he wanted it to be.

No sooner had he laid his hand on the car door to open it when he came to a halt. He could feel his skin prickling, the hairs on the back of his neck standing on edge, and a heightened state of alertness took over him. Something wasn't right. He scanned the area around him, but he couldn't place what it was. Everything still seemed to be in place. There was no movement around him, only the rustling of the breeze through the trees. He'd always been told to trust his gut, and his gut was telling him the necklace could wait. Something was off, and he couldn't quite place it.

He moved towards the front of the inn, always looking for something out of place. The only bedroom that was lit was Brigid's, which made perfect sense because they had no bookings for the weekend. He moved around the back of the inn. There was a small stream of light coming from Ailbe's office. He remembered Ailbe saying to him at the party that he had to finish something at the inn before heading home. No doubt he'd fallen asleep at his desk again.

He was about to circle back around to the front of the inn when there was a stronger gust of wind, blowing the back door open and slamming it shut again. Except it didn't close fully. Surely, Ailbe hadn't forgotten to lock the door. As far as he could tell, Ailbe looked after this place like it was his own castle. He always did his rounds—oftentimes more than once. Alex moved to the door and pushed it open to go inside, startling as something rattled across the floor. He flicked the light switch on and realised what it was—the lock was broken. If this was someone's sick idea of a joke...

He closed the door, pushing a trolley up against it to stop anyone from coming in—it would have to wait until tomorrow to be fixed—and scanned the kitchen. Nothing seemed to be missing, but then, he wasn't as familiar with the kitchen as the rest of the inn. He added getting Ailbe to check over the kitchen in the morning to his mental list of things to do. He sighed. Maybe that's what didn't feel right, but he still couldn't shake the feeling. Then, he heard it. A scream so terrifying and sickening that it made his heart sink. It rattled through the inn, filling every room.

Brigid.

He raced out of the kitchen to the base of the stairs, grabbing a floorboard that was waiting to be placed, and Ailbe stumbled out of his office, terror on his face.

'Where be the banshee?' he said, drawing out his words, an almost empty bottle of whiskey in his hand.

Alex shook his head. This was the first time he'd seen Ailbe drinking, and he had no time to worry about mythological creatures. 'It's Brigid, Ailbe,' he said, taking the stairs two at a time. 'Call the police.'

That seemed to sober him up, since he headed for the phone at the reception desk. Confident Ailbe wasn't so drunk he didn't know what he was doing, he pushed against Brigid's door. *Locked*.

'Shoot,' he mumbled.

Keys—he needed keys. He ran his hands through

his pockets, relieved to find Brigid's keys. He fumbled with the metal, shoving it into the lock and turning, nudging the door open when he heard the *click*. But when he saw her slumped against the wall, blood on her clothes, her breaths shallow and racking her body, the only thing he could hear was the click of the lock ringing through his head.

'Brigid!' he yelled, dropping the plank, and racing over to her. 'Oh, God, Brigid!'

Her face was pained, her mouth moving, but nothing but her shallow breath coming out. He thought he could make out a name whispered on her breath, but his heart was pounding so hard he could hear it in his eardrums. He shrugged off his shirt—still unbuttoned—and rolled it up, pressing it to her stomach to stop the bleeding.

'Hold on, Brigid,' he said, panic in his voice. 'Stay with me.'

He reached for her arm, but she shrugged him off, her expression more terrified than he'd ever seen on anyone's face.

'D... ar... cy!' she forced through her teeth.

Darcy. God, he swore if that bastard did this... He looked into her eyes, misted from pain and tears, and saw movement that shouldn't be there. They weren't alone. He watched the reflection in her eyes as the figure moved closer, a glint of something in his hand raising slowly. He gritted his teeth, his fists balled.

'You son of a bitch.'

Alex swung his leg out, swiping Darcy's feet from

under him, satisfied he'd fallen to the ground. But it wasn't over yet. With Darcy on the ground, Alex used his weight to hold him down, battling with his hands, his eyes on the knife stained with Brigid's blood.

'She's only using you!' Darcy spat. 'I did us both a favour.'

'Shut the *hell* up!' Alex yelled, forcing his forearm against Darcy's neck.

The plank was just out of reach, but he still had the knife to worry about. He couldn't let go of either of Darcy's hands without giving him an advantage. But he had to do something. He shifted his weight and brought his knee up, colliding with Darcy's side. Darcy winced, but Alex didn't stop. Blow after blow. He released the hand that wasn't wielding the knife and aimed at his nose. If he'd broken Darcy's nose on that first day, then another blow to it should hurt like hell.

Sure enough, Darcy cried out in pain, but his jerk threw Alex off balance—a strength he could only get from a mixture of adrenaline and alcohol and whatever the hell else he was taking. Alex swore for not thinking to take any external influences into account. But then again, his wife was bleeding out and he was literally fighting for his life—for their lives—and the longer he took to get rid of Darcy, the less chance Brigid had of surviving. The reality of his situation hit him hard and fuelled his fire.

Darcy was on his feet, staggering, searching for the knife he'd somehow managed to lose. Still on the ground, Alex could see the glint of it under the bed.

But he sure as hell wasn't going to bring it back into the fight. He pulled himself into a crouch and leapt towards Darcy, pulling him back to the ground. He could see fists flying and feel the connections—some his, some Darcy's. It was all happening so quickly he could barely tell which was which. At one stage, he'd had him pinned beneath him, another stalemate and battle of the hands.

He heard Brigid cough—a raspy, choking cough—and fear rushed through him. He glanced up to see Brigid slump a little lower, the blood draining from her face. He had no more time. But that brief moment was all Darcy needed to get the upper hand, flipping them to a reversed position, his hands around Alex's neck, his eyes wild. No mercy.

'Two in the hand is better than one in the bush, right?' Darcy spat, squeezing his hands tighter.

Alex grappled at Darcy's wrist, but it was a losing battle. He was going to die in his great-uncle's inn next to his wife. And Darcy would likely get away with it. He should have seen this coming. He should have thought something was wrong when he didn't hear the *click* of the lock when he and Brigid came into her room. He'd thought it was strange the door wasn't locked, but he'd thought Brigid might have forgotten to lock it. But that wasn't Brigid. She double-checked everything. She'd been jumping at just about any noise all week—he'd noticed it. Had she suspected Darcy would do something like this? Why wouldn't she tell him?

Just as his vision started to blur and his body was

crying out for oxygen, he heard a *crack* and felt the hold loosen. He felt the oxygen rushing into his body, pushing him into a coughing fit, and he saw Ailbe standing above him, the plank in his hand, and Darcy unconscious on the floor next to him.

'I'll deal with him,' Ailbe said, knowing in his eyes. 'Get Brigid to the hospital.'

'Thank you, Ailbe,' he croaked, his voice hoarse from the trauma.

He staggered to his feet and rushed over to Brigid, mustering every bit of strength he could. She was still breathing, but her breaths were shallow and raspy. She was unconscious.

'Brigid! Come on, stay with me!' he yelled.

There was no response. Feeling a surge of adrenaline, he scooped her up in his arms and raced her out the door, down the stairs, and out to the car. He laid her down in the backseat of his car and jumped in the driver's seat, praying to God he'd make it to the hospital in time. He could hear the sirens of the police cars heading towards the inn. A few quick turns and the hospital was in sight, but Brigid's breathing was growing weaker by the second. He screeched the car to a stop in front of the emergency entry and was lifting her out quicker than he could blink.

'Help!' he yelled, racing her in through the doors.

The nurses nearby looked shocked for a moment, then switched into action, yelling orders at everyone nearby. Someone pulled a gurney in front of him and he lowered her onto the bed. God, she looked so pale. So helpless. The pink of her soft lips started to look blue against her skin and her long eyelashes rested against her cheeks. The same lips he may never be able to kiss again, and the same cheeks he may never be able to touch again.

'She's critical.'

'She needs blood.'

'Two stab wounds to the stomach.'

'We're losing her!'

He couldn't tell who was saying what, but he watched helplessly as the medical staff hooked her up to oxygen and started rushing her off towards theatre.

'What's her blood type?' One of the nurses directed the question to him.

'I—' He couldn't speak. He was scared to death that his wife was going to die. He didn't know anything about her—not even her blood type—and yet he couldn't imagine life without her. 'I don't know,' he stammered.

'We'll give her universal blood,' she said, noting it on a chart. 'Allergies?'

He shook his head. He could feel his skin growing clammy. She was going to die. And he knew nothing that could save her. 'I don't—'

'He's in shock,' she said, grabbing another nurse by the arm. 'See to him.'

God, there was something Brigid had told him. Allergies...

'No,' he called after the nurse who was asking him questions. 'Anti-inflammatory drugs—she's allergic.'

The nurse nodded. 'Just as well you remembered.'

The nurse disappeared behind the same doors they had taken Brigid through and he collapsed onto a nearby seat, cradling his head in his hands. For the first time in his life, he felt truly alone, helpless. He'd always had something to do, something to keep his hands busy, and someone to be there for him. Someone brought him a glass of water and took Brigid's basic details from him—even saying they'll call her daddy and Colleen for him. God, he didn't look forward to that reunion.

How was a man to tell his in-laws his wife had been stabbed by her ex and the father of her child, the night after they'd eloped?

***

'You bastard!'

Alex stepped back while Colleen held onto her daddy's arm. He'd already been in a lethal fight tonight. He wasn't ready for another, especially with Brigid's daddy. Not with his wife behind a set of doors with half the emergency staff fighting to keep her alive.

'You waltz into town thinking you can have whatever you want,' Mr Murphy spat, shrugging Colleen off his arm, and pushing his finger against Alex's chest. 'Steal Brigid from us, fooling her with whatever smooth talking you're capable of, and get her stabbed. What the hell were you thinking?'

'I was thinking she was safe,' he said through gritted teeth. He didn't want to pick a fight, but he also wasn't going to let anyone make him out as some selfish asshole. 'And I didn't smooth talk Brigid into anything. How was I to know her ex was a psycho bent on vengeance?'

Mr Murphy's face paled, his lip twitching. Colleen tried to get his attention, but he ignored her. 'What did you just say?' he said.

'Who do you think stabbed her?' Alex said, standing tall. 'I sure as hell didn't. I wouldn't do anything to hurt her—ever—and I've already told you that. Darcy's the one who stabbed her.' He glanced over at Colleen. How much did they know? He knew Mr Murphy didn't know Brigid was pregnant. But would Brigid have shared it with Colleen? Her eyes were wide. 'He ... wasn't happy ... about our union.'

'He's not the only one.'

'Daddy,' Colleen said, a hint of warning in her voice.

'I'm sorry you didn't get to parade your daughter in front of everyone,' Alex said. 'But did you ever think maybe that's not what Brigid wanted?'

'Are you saying it was Brigid's idea to elope?' His face was going red.

'*Daddy*.'

'I'm saying we wouldn't have done it if either of us didn't want it. The least you could do is support her in her decisions instead of exiling her. Do you know how upset she was about that? Everyone came to the party except for you. She was heartbroken—her own father couldn't be proud of her for five minutes. If anyone's to blame, it's you.'

Maybe he shouldn't have said the last bit, but it was too late to take it back anyway. Besides, it was true. Things could have been different if Mr Murphy had just supported Brigid and her decisions from the start.

'She didn't get stabbed on my watch,' he growled.

'No, because you'd turned your back on that responsibility,' he said. 'You're the one who tried to push them together in the first place. This wouldn't have happened if you'd just let her be.'

'Are you questioning my parenting methods?'

'*I* would never turn my back on my child.'

'Guys!' Colleen stood between them. 'Stop acting like idiots. Brigid is fighting for her life behind those doors and you two playing the blame game isn't going to help her.' She turned towards Alex. 'Yes, you screwed up. You should have at least told us you were planning to elope. But for God knows what reason, Brigid decided we didn't need to know. Probably because she knew you—' she turned to Mr Murphy. '—wouldn't have agreed to it because you can't stand the idea of one of us going out on our own and actually making a go of it.'

'Colleen,' Mr Murphy said sternly.

'No, Daddy,' she continued. 'Listen to me. You've never been proud of Brigid, and if you have, you have a weird way of showing it. You have such high expectations of us that we can't live up to. Ever since Mammy died. Now, my sister, your daughter, and Alex's wife needs us to get along, and that's exactly what I plan to do.'

'Excuse me, Mr Carter?' Alex turned to see one of the people who had been tending to Brigid when he brought her in standing behind them. 'I hope I'm not interrupting anything. I'm the surgeon who was working on Brigid.' He glanced at Colleen and Mr Murphy. 'Are you relatives?'

'Yes, they are,' Alex answered. 'Is she okay?'

'We've done everything we can,' the surgeon said. 'She'd lost a lot of blood and there was extensive damage. But she's stable now. If you hadn't brought her in when you did, it would have been too late. We're keeping a close eye on her for now, but we're hopeful.'

'Thank you, doctor,' Colleen said.

Mr Murphy took a seat in the waiting room with Colleen, but Alex followed the surgeon down the hall.

'Sorry but can I—' he started. 'Is the ... umm ... is the baby all right?'

The surgeon furrowed his brow. 'Mr Carter, there was no baby.'

The words hit him like a brick being thrown at him. No baby? Had Darcy somehow...

'No,' Alex said. 'Brigid's pregnant. How could there be no baby?'

'Trust me, Alex,' he said, placing a hand on his

shoulder. 'I was just operating on her. If anyone could tell you she was pregnant, it's me. There was no baby. There was no pregnancy.'

Alex watched as the surgeon continued down the hallway, his heart pounding in his chest. Had Brigid known she wasn't pregnant? Had it all been some kind of ploy? But if it was, why the hell would Darcy be so adamant to end it? He'd propositioned a marriage of convenience because he knew she needed help. And now it turns out she never needed an arrangement. If she knew, why would she have agreed to marry him? Sure, he would have preferred the child to be his instead of some bastard's anyway. But he was willing to take that child on as his own.

The child that didn't exist.

Because Brigid was never pregnant.

Chapter 17

She could see him—the wild look in his eyes, the growl in his voice as he spoke. She could still feel the horror she felt when she tried to warn Alex that Darcy was behind him, his knife held high, but no words came out. She'd imagined herself yelling for him to watch out, but all she could hear was a wheeze escaping through her lips. She'd never been more terrified in her life than she was when she thought Darcy was going to kill Alex.

She'd tried to will her body to move—to help him—but the searing pain in her stomach was crippling. She could still feel the wet of her blood between her fingers. She remembered drifting in and out of consciousness, but the final thing she saw before slipping into darkness was Alex on the floor with Darcy's hands around his neck. She knew that was it. That was the end. Their story was over. They were both dead.

So why the hell did those images keep flashing through her mind and she found herself just as immobile and helpless as she had when it was happening? And why could she still feel the numbing pain in her stomach and the mumbling of voices she didn't recognise?

Is that what it's like to die? Is life after death filled with agony and reliving your final moments? Surely, not. It couldn't be. There had to be an end.

It couldn't be like this.

***

Alex rested his head in his hands. Mr Murphy had long gone for work, seemingly content Colleen would stay and let him know when Brigid woke up. Even though Alex couldn't understand how Brigid's daddy could focus on work or carry on as usual after his daughter narrowly escaped death, he was also relieved he didn't have to deal with Mr Murphy staring daggers at him.

Colleen had managed to put a stop to their spat, but Alex knew when he wasn't liked. And Mr Murphy didn't like him. He blamed Alex for everything— tricking Brigid into marrying him, coming between the relationship they had, getting her stabbed. But Alex knew otherwise. Alex knew Brigid's relationship with her daddy was like treading on thin ice, and

Brigid might not have been stabbed if she'd never been with Darcy. But Colleen was right—there was no point playing the blame game because what happened, happened. The past can't be changed, so there was no point in dwelling on whose fault it was. They just had to focus on how they were going to move forward with what they had.

And right now, his wife needed him. She needed *them*. And he needed her.

He'd never been as terrified as he was when he thought Brigid was going to die. What they had was so new—they barely knew each other. It wasn't the thought that he could have become a widower after being married for a day that terrified him. It was the thought of living without Brigid, never knowing what they could have had. Never having a family with her.

But now he knew she was never pregnant, he couldn't stop the niggling thought at the back of his mind. Did she know? Surely, she must have believed she was pregnant. But wouldn't she have done tests? Those things are pretty accurate now, aren't they? How could she not know she wasn't pregnant?

A part of him told him that it's quite plausible— it's a small town and she didn't want anyone to find out, so never got the tests. Also, why would she lie about being pregnant if Darcy was willing to go as far as he did to get rid of it? But maybe it was the timing. Did she know about the money Carrick had left for Alex along with the inn? From what he knew, Ailbe was the only one who knew. But Brigid did basically run the inn …

Alex groaned into his hands. He couldn't let himself think Brigid was after the money—especially not when she couldn't defend herself. Besides, she wasn't that kind of person, was she? And even if she was, *he* was the one who suggested they get married, not her. Colleen cleared her throat.

'Alex,' she said.

He looked up at her, wondering how long she'd been sitting across from him in the waiting room. He knew she'd gone to get a coffee, but he hadn't even registered she'd returned. She looked concerned.

'I—' she started, glancing down at the takeaway coffee cup in her hands. 'I know about—' She let out a shaky breath. 'Well … the reason why you and Brigid got married.'

Alex squinted, looking at her questioningly. He didn't want to say anything until he knew how much she knew—and whether or not it was true.

'About the … baby,' she said. 'Brigid told me when she realised she was. She said she'd find a way to handle the situation, I just … I guess I didn't put two and two together until now.'

'Does he—?'

'Daddy?' she shook her head. 'No, he doesn't know. And I won't tell him. But I just—' She glanced away again. 'I can't stop wondering if … if the baby is all right.'

Alex felt that push on his heart again. Brigid wasn't pregnant. She never had been. But was it really his place to tell Colleen when Brigid may not even know it herself? He shook his head slowly.

'I don't know,' he said.

She sighed, staring down at her cup again. 'For the record,' she said. 'I don't agree with Daddy. I mean, yes, I was a bit … upset … you guys got married without telling me. But I think you're all right, Alex, which is a lot nicer than anything I could ever say about Darcy. Even if you've only known Brigid for two weeks.'

'What makes you think that?' Had Brigid told her that as well?

Colleen scoffed. 'Oh, please,' she said. 'You really expect me to believe she met you two months ago and kept in touch? She would have told me. I'm not as easily fooled as you might think, Alex, but I get it. You had to lie to make Daddy believe it.' She leaned back against her seat. 'But I'm glad she found you. Even at the dinner, I could see you cared more about her than Darcy was ever capable of. Just remember if you ever hurt her, I will personally make you suffer for it.'

A smile tugged at his lips. 'Noted,' he said.

So, at least he had Colleen's approval. But he understood she might have to act differently around their daddy. God, if he could just talk some sense into him …

'Mr Carter?'

Alex looked up at the nurse, his breath caught in his throat.

'Brigid's awake,' she continued. 'You can come see her now.'

He exhaled, relief washing over his body. She was

awake. She was okay. She was on the road to recovery. He glanced over at Colleen. She waved her hand at him.

'Go on,' she said. 'I'll let Daddy know.'

***

Brigid stared at the end of her bed. So, she didn't die. Not quite. But she'd come close. She'd stared death in the eye and, somehow, she survived. She could still feel the ache in her stomach, despite the painkillers she was on, and she could barely move without assistance, but she'd be okay. But what gave her even more relief than knowing she'd survived, was Alex walking through the door of her room with nothing more than a slightly swollen lip and a bit of bruising on his neck. They were both alive. Darcy hadn't won.

Alex bent down and swept a kiss against her cheek before pulling a seat up close to the bed and sitting down. He took her hand in his, pressing another soft kiss against the back of her fingers.

'Wha—how did you … Darcy?'

She wasn't sure if it was the drugs making her somewhat incoherent, or if she was in shock. Alex's lips pulled to the side, his smile making the swelling less obvious.

'Ailbe whacked him over the back of the head with a plank,' he said, his eyes flashing. 'Knocked him out. He's being held in custody until he's trialled. He's going to jail, Brigid, I'll make sure of it. I thought

I was—' He reached out to her and rubbed his thumb across her cheek. 'I thought I was going to lose you.'

She squeezed his hand, her eyes clouding with unshed tears. 'But you didn't.'

A shadow crept across his face and his eyes darkened, a look which sent a shiver down her spine. 'I wanted to kill him for hurting you, Brigid.' His words racked through her body. 'I had to work so hard to not give in to that.'

'Alex,' she said, not much over a whisper.

He shook his head. 'I wanted to be around for you, Brigid. I *promised* you. I couldn't let myself do anything that would land me in jail.'

She blinked back the tears. 'I couldn't have chosen a better man for us.'

She'd thought it might have made him smile, but she wasn't prepared for the opposite to happen. He furrowed his brow, his lips turned into a frown.

'Us?'

She nodded. 'Me,' she said. 'And the … baby.'

Even as she said it, she felt the heaviness in her chest. She pressed her hand to her stomach and felt the twinge of pain. She lifted her shirt to see the dressing and the realisation washed over her. Darcy had stabbed her. Twice. Alex had brought her to the hospital, and she'd had surgery. Surgery that saved her life. *The baby*.

'Brigid,' Alex said quietly, squeezing her hand tighter.

'Mrs Carter, I'm glad to see you're recovering.' The lady she assumed was her doctor came to a halt next to her bed and checked the numbers on the machines she was hooked up to.

'The baby,' she whispered.

The doctor's eyes widened, and she sighed. 'Mr Carter did mention you were both under the impression that you're pregnant.'

'No, I am,' she said, desperately. 'I missed my … I'm late.'

'When was your last period?'

'Six weeks ago, maybe seven.'

'Did you get a pregnancy test done to confirm it?'

Brigid shook her head. 'I—' She what? She didn't think of it? She didn't want to raise suspicion in a town where word spread until she knew what to do about it? She'd never been late before. Wasn't the likely thing that she was pregnant?

The doctor sat on the end of her bed and took Brigid's hand in hers. 'Brigid, it's not uncommon for a woman to be late or skip a period altogether. Especially when they're stressed or have only recently become sexually active. Hormones are to blame for that.'

'You mean—'

'There's no baby, Brigid. You're not pregnant.' The doctor took a shaky breath. 'Which makes this next part a whole lot more difficult to say.'

'What do you mean?' Alex asked.

She felt something tighten in her throat, making it difficult to breathe. Or maybe it was that her breaths were choppy and uneven—she couldn't tell for sure.

'Brigid,' she started, squeezing her hand. 'The stab wounds—there was significant damage. We did our best to patch it up, but it doesn't change the outcome. It will result in a lot of scar tissue which, unfortunately, will make it very difficult, if not impossible, for you to conceive. And if by some miracle you did, the pregnancy would be unlikely to hold. I'm sorry, Brigid. Alex.'

Everything blurred around her, her eyes only able to focus briefly on Alex and the shocked look he had before looking away. There was a ringing piercing through her ears as though a bombshell just exploded nearby, and her heart felt like it had been ripped from her chest and crushed mercilessly in front of her. Heartbroken. The only time she'd ever come close to feeling like this was when her mammy died. But this—this was different.

She wasn't pregnant.

Not to Darcy. Not to Alex. Not to anyone. Should she feel relieved about that? If that was all the doctor had told her, it would have given her and Alex time to plan and prepare. But it isn't just that she's not pregnant. She will *never* have a child of her own. Her plans to one day have a family with Alex, children of their own. Shattered.

It could have all been avoided. If she'd just had the courage to simply get a pregnancy test when she first suspected it instead of taking a late period as a given, she would have known. Darcy wouldn't have stabbed her. Alex wouldn't have married her. Alex, the man who she'd been falling in love with and won't be able to give him children. Would he still look at her the same? Would he regret marrying her now he knew what their future held?

Would she be able to wake up to him every day knowing she couldn't give him everything?

Could she even look him in the eye without her heart breaking?

***

He couldn't begin to understand how Brigid might feel. Clearly, she was convinced she was pregnant. It wasn't a ploy. Which made him feel even worse for even thinking it might have been. It had to be the rollercoaster of emotions. She'd almost died—they both could have died. It was only natural for his brain to try to think up some kind of paranoid excuse for the whole not-pregnant thing when Brigid couldn't be there to set his mind at ease.

But this—her reaction to finding out she wasn't pregnant. The look she had. It wasn't the look someone who was up to something had. It was the look of someone who just had her heart broken. He felt so stupid that he'd even entertained the idea that she might not have been honest with him. She had—well, as much as she could be. She hadn't had any tests done to confirm the pregnancy. She was acting on suspicion. They'd married under *suspicion* of being pregnant. Now Brigid knew she wasn't pregnant, did she plan on hightailing it out of their relationship?

He'd had time to process the fact that she wasn't pregnant before the doctor delivered the news that she couldn't have kids. Yet, the news still shocked him to his core. He'd heard about it. He'd known people who'd said they couldn't have kids. He'd never known how traumatising it was to hear the news first-hand. He'd never thought it could ever happen to them. To put it simply, he was devastated. For him, for Brigid, for their future. He couldn't even begin to imagine how Brigid felt.

He watched her expression change as she shut down. Her face was wet from tears, but she looked like she had no control over it. Heck, he was probably crying without realising it. As the doctor left, he slid onto the bed next to Brigid and pulled her into his arms, rocking and shushing her until her sobs eased and her tears dried up and she entered a state of emotional numbness. Then, he held her, stroking her hair until she fell asleep, feeling the same numbness she no doubt felt. Except his was fuelled with something more.

Darcy did this.

Brigid might not have been pregnant. But Darcy made it so she'd never be able to conceive again. Darcy broke Brigid—shattered her into a million pieces that Alex was desperately trying to hold together. Darcy ruined her life. And for that, he deserved to spend the rest of his life rotting in jail.

And Alex wouldn't stop until he made sure he did.

Chapter 18

It had been six and a half weeks since Darcy stabbed Brigid. And even though she was recovering well physically, Alex could tell she still had a long way to go. He'd divided his time between Brigid, making sure Darcy got what he deserved, and working overtime on the inn. It would have made sense that he worked less on the inn, and he'd tried it for the first two weeks when Brigid needed his help the most. But as she started being able to do some things by herself again, he needed something to distract him. He started working on the inn at the crack of dawn, and went well into the night, every day for the past month. He was exhausted. And he didn't like waiting. He'd been fighting with tooth and nail to make sure Darcy got the maximum sentence he could get. And now, it was at the end and he and Brigid would be able to get on with their lives. At least, for a while.

'It's done,' he said, shrugging his jacket off.

'Aye?' Ailbe looked up from his paperwork as Alex stood in the doorway. 'What be the sentence?'

'Life imprisonment. The bastard deserves it.'

'Aye,' Ailbe said, nodding. Alex let out a sigh, though he couldn't be certain if it was from relief or concern. 'Yer not happy 'bout it?'

'I am,' he said, feeling as though he was trying to convince himself more than Ailbe. 'Of course I am. I just … I know a life sentence doesn't necessarily mean he'll be in jail for his whole life. His sentence will be reviewed many times and no doubt him and his family will keep fighting for him to get out. It's good, for now, but it's not certain.'

Ailbe nodded, rubbing the whiskers on his chin with his hand. Alex noticed he looked wearier than usual with bags under his eyes and his hair scruffy. He looked … unkempt. Stressed.

'It's always a worry,' Ailbe said, staring at the paperwork. 'I been worried about it m'self.'

'I mean, I'll never stop fighting to keep him in jail,' Alex continued. 'But Brigid doesn't need the stress. It should just be done and dusted. She shouldn't have to worry that the man who tried to kill her might be roaming the streets again. She's already got too much on her plate.'

'I understand. But at least ye know she's safe fer now.'

Alex sighed, crossing his arms over his chest. 'I guess you're right,' he said, studying Ailbe. 'Now, do we need to talk about caring for you, too, Al?'

'What do ye mean?' Ailbe's eyes had a fire burning in them. 'I'm fine.'

'No offence, Al, but you look terrible.'

A smile tugged at Ailbe's lips and he erupted into a bellied laughter. 'Probably the same reason as ye. We been workin' our asses off because we can't function right without her.' Ailbe's face grew solemn.

Alex knew it was a sensitive topic for Ailbe, but he also couldn't let him blame himself for what happened. 'Al, it's not your fault. Nothing could have stopped Darcy.'

Ailbe shook his head and swiped at a tear spilling from his left eye, sniffing loudly. 'It was me job to check the doors. Make sure ev'ryone were safe. I don't get drunk, Mr Carter, not usually. It was jest me daddy's anniversary—when he died—ye know? I still … it gets to me, every year.'

Alex nodded understandably. 'We both have a day, Al.'

Ailbe's eyes widened as he looked up at Alex. 'Yer daddy?'

'And my mum,' he said. 'Twice a year, I could probably be found in a similar state to what you were in. There's no shame in remembering them.' Ailbe nodded, pressing his lips together, his chin quivering. 'Brigid doesn't blame you, Ailbe. And my bets are that Darcy planned that day knowing the factors—all of them. It couldn't just be a coincidence.'

'Yer probably right,' Ailbe said solemnly, staring at the paperwork in front of him.

Alex knew he was right. Ailbe was a loved man in the community. He was sure Darcy would have known when the anniversary of Ailbe's daddy's death was, especially if he'd been having a relationship with Brigid for as long as they had. No, he would have known. He would have known it was the one day of the year Ailbe got drunk. He would have figured Ailbe was passed out by the time he'd come around. He would have known the inn didn't have any bookings for that weekend because of the windows being delivered. Darcy had his nose in everything—he would have known that. The only person Darcy would have had to worry about was Alex. And he probably hadn't expected he was going to sleep with Brigid that night. But one thing was for certain. Darcy had had eyes on Brigid, planning his chance and the perfect moment to get to her. And Alex wished he'd known before Darcy had a chance to do anything.

There was a knock against the open door and Alex turned to see Lee standing behind him, a puzzled look on his face.

'Alex, there's someone here to see you.'

Alex squinted. He didn't have a delivery set for that day and he still hadn't made friends with many people in the town.

'Who is it?' he asked.

Lee shook his head, shrugging his shoulders. 'She

wouldn't tell me her name. But I know she's not from around here.'

She? Could it …? No, it couldn't be. Alex followed Lee out to the front of the inn and saw her standing near the fireplace. She had his back towards him, but there was no mistaking the brown bob she'd styled her hair as before he left. What the hell was she doing here? He stopped in his steps and folded his arms over his chest. He nodded to Lee and waited until he'd left the room. Then, he cleared his throat. The woman turned on her heel and smiled at him. The broad, flirtatious smile he'd once fallen for, but never again.

'Hi, Alex.'

***

Brigid ran her fingers over the red lines on her stomach, looking at her reflection in the mirror. Scars. A reminder that will stay with her forever of what she won't be able to have because of Darcy. She'd gotten Alex's message about Darcy's sentence. She should be happy about that, right? But it was as though she felt … numb. She'd spent the past six weeks cooped up in her room, staring out the window, staring at the wall. At her scars. Anything. But it seemed that in anything she looked at, it couldn't take her mind off the fact that she'd never be able to bear a child.

At first, she'd been devastated. How could one hear that kind of news and not feel that way? Then, she'd been angry at herself for not getting a simple test done, followed by a series of 'what if's'. What if she knew she wasn't pregnant? Would she have married Alex? Would she still be with Darcy, oblivious of the maniac he had hidden beneath his skin? What if there was something else wrong with her that made her late and unable to have children anyway? Then, she'd entered a state of numbness. Nothing made her smile the way she used to. Nothing amused her the way it did. Everything just seemed … superfluous … superficial. Nothing had the same kind of importance to her that it used to. All she could feel was grief for the child who never existed, and loss for the children she'd never have.

Alex had been there for her the whole time— caring for her, bringing her food, helping her with everything—but she hadn't been the easiest patient to deal with. She'd spent the weeks in a horrible mood, swapping between silence and sarcasm. She'd lost count of how many times she'd said something to Alex that he probably took the wrong way. Honestly, it had sounded significantly harsher than she'd wanted it to. She'd seen the cut look on his face when she'd said something mean. She'd seen his lips tighten and his Adam's apple move up and down as though he was swallowing words he didn't want to say. And sure, it made her feel bad. But she couldn't let herself feel close to anyone. Because when you let someone in, you're giving them the power to hurt you, and you give others the power to ruin you.

But six weeks was a lot of time to think and process. And even though she hadn't shown her face downstairs in that time except to go to appointments, she was ready to now. She felt ready to apologise to Alex for being so rude while she processed and healed. She was ready to distract herself with menial tasks that she was able to do again. Being stuck in a room left to her thoughts made her feel like she was going around in circles in her head. She wasn't sure she could take it much longer. She might be far from healed mentally, but she was ready to start moving on.

And preferably with Alex, if he hadn't changed his mind about her. He'd seen her at her worst. And she wasn't sure she could get any worse than that. But now, a big part of their arrangement had become irrelevant. And she would understand if he didn't want to be with her anymore.

Even if it broke her heart.

She pulled on her loose-fitting shirt to hide the scars and slipped her jacket on. She took the stairs slowly, holding on to the rail in case her stomach twinged. Ailbe met her at the bottom of the stairs, a smile on his face.

'Good to see yer on the mend, lass,' he said, pulling her into a hug when she reached him.

'Oh, Al,' she said. 'I figured it was time to get back to work and sort you all out.'

He laughed and shook his head, his smile uncontrollable. 'So good to see ye. The way Mr Carter was talkin' made it seem like ye'd burrowed yerself into a hole and refused to come out.'

She was sure it was a bit of an exaggeration on Ailbe's part—she'd heard him use metaphors like that about many things. But she wouldn't blame Alex if he was the one who came up with that particular one. She *had* burrowed herself into a metaphorical hole. She *had* refused to start moving on with her life. She sighed, shaking the thoughts from her mind. She may not have been ready for it then, but she was doing something about it now.

'Speaking of Alex, do you know where he is?' she said. 'I need to talk to him to … apologise … for being so difficult to manage.'

'Aye,' Ailbe said, rubbing his whiskered chin with his hand. 'Saw him go outside. Said he had to deal with somethin'. Some lass showed up. Think he said her name was Betty. But I tell ye somethin'—she ain't look like she'd be up to any good. Sh—oh.' He scrunched his nose up. 'I said too much, didn't I?'

Brigid closed her eyes and shook her head, hoping the movement might bring the blood back to her face. *Betty*? As in, Alex's ex who left him for another man Betty? Surely, Ailbe misheard, right? It couldn't be her. Alex had assured her it was well and truly over between them. Why would she have travelled from Paris to Kinsale to see him?

'Lass?'

She opened her eyes to see the worried look on Ailbe's face. She patted him on the shoulder. 'No, Ailbe,' she said. 'You've said just enough. I'll just, umm … see if he needs anything.'

She heard Ailbe mumbling something, but she couldn't make out the words. Or rather, she wasn't focussed on what he was saying. Her feet carried her as quick as she could manage to the front door of the inn. She took a deep breath and stepped outside, scanning the garden before landing her eyes near the large tree to the left. And her husband lip-locked with a short-haired brunette sporting a visible bump on her stomach.

It must have been for one or two seconds she watched—enough to take a shaky breath and feel the little bit of her heart she'd put back together shatter again. So, that's Betty. And she was pregnant. Presumably with Alex's child, if the way she kissed him was any indication. She spun on her heel, barging inside and up the stairs, ignoring Ailbe's calls to see if she was all right. Because she wasn't. But she couldn't admit it to anyone. She grabbed her suitcase and started loading her clothes into it, occasionally swiping at the tears that were flowing freely.

Alex had moved on.

Or back. Whichever it was. He obviously still loved Betty and clearly had unfinished business with her. And maybe he should go back to her. She was *pregnant*—something Brigid would never be. He could have a family with Betty. Brigid could never compete with that. Brigid was broken, wounded, and had a temper Alex would surely tire of. She could never give Alex a family. She had nothing to offer him. She'd thought she could love him—she'd thought she did. But he'd broken his promise to be faithful to her by kissing that hussy. Oh, God, what if she moved here to be with him? Could Brigid deal with that?

She zipped the suitcase up and rolled it off her bed, cringing at the pain in her side, but she moved on. She had to move on. Otherwise, she wouldn't get up again.

***

Alex didn't move his lips when Betty kissed him. If he did, she would think there was a chance. But he'd learned how to push Betty away when he suspected she was seeing someone else. He did, however, take hold of her shoulders and pull her away from him.

'What the *hell* are you doing, Betty?'

He kept his tone flat. No emotion. Because he had none—not for Betty. He'd wasted too much time on her already. If it wasn't for her screwing him over for so long, he could have been in Kinsale earlier. He could have met Brigid earlier—the one woman who he was convinced he actually wanted to spend the rest of his life with, despite … well … everything.

Betty's mouth dropped open. 'I thought … I—'

He shook his head. 'What did you think? That you could fly to Ireland, show up on my doorstep and everything would be all right? You could have another chance of screwing with me?'

'I thought you'd at least hear me out.'

She propped her hands on her hips, her jacket

parting. And that's when he saw it—the bump—and he felt like he'd been kicked in the chest. 'How long?'

'Twenty weeks.' She folded her arms across her chest, sighing, her expression softening. 'It's yours.'

'Bullshit.'

His? She seriously thought he would believe that? 'Alex—'

'No, seriously, Betty. How long did you have to convince yourself that I would buy that?'

'I *am* serious, Alex.'

He shook his head. 'We never once had unprotected sex. Clearly can't say the same for the other guy you were with. What happened to him, by the way? Wouldn't he be interested to know he's going to be a dad?'

Betty's lips tightened, and her eyes narrowed—a look he knew well. 'I ended it with him. He wasn't … you. And there was that time we had the accident.'

Alex scoffed. 'Accident?'

Betty averted her eyes. 'You know, the mishap we had? About, I don't know, twenty weeks ago?'

Alex squinted at her. 'We never had a mishap, Betty.'

She waved her hand at him. 'Oh, you were probably too drunk to remember.'

He raised an eyebrow. 'No, I *wish* I was drunk. But I never had more than one drink at a time for the whole time we were together.'

'I don't know, Alex. I just know it's definitely yours.'

Alex studied her eyes. Was she truly convinced it

was his? His guess was the other guy got scared about having a baby and ran off. He wouldn't be the only bastard Alex knew of who didn't want to deal with having a baby.

'I want a paternity test done.'

'What?'

'You think I'm the father, I know I'm not. So, there's only one way to know for sure.'

'O—all right. We can … do that.'

'Another thing.'

'Mmm?'

'Don't show up here again.' He might have sounded rude, but he didn't care. This was just a speed bump he had to get over to move on with Brigid.

'But I—' she stammered. 'I think we should get back together if the baby is yours.'

'I'm going to make this very clear, Betty, and I'm only going to say it once, so listen carefully. We are *never* getting back together. Do you understand that? I'm married now, and I love *her*. So, get used to it.'

Her mouth dropped open and she snapped it closed, her eyes glistening and blinking more than usual. 'You—you're married?'

'Yes, I am. And you're not going to come between me and Brigid—I won't allow it. So, I suggest that as soon as we have the results for the paternity test, you jump on the plane you came here on and go home.'

'What if it's yours?'

Her eyes challenged him, but he wasn't going to let her have one on him. He brought his face close to hers—inches apart—and when he spoke, it was more of a growl than anything.

'*If* it's mine, my suggestion remains the same.'

He heard the door of the inn slam shut and heard the roll of a suitcase, keys dangling, and felt his heart drop. He turned to see Brigid walking towards her car, her head down. But he could see in her body language that she was pissed. Had she seen Betty kiss him? God, it was just his luck that the day his wife decided to leave her room, his ex showed up.

'Brigid!' he called out. Why was she leaving?

She paused at the car and, without looking back at him, she flipped him off. *Shoot.*

'Oh, yes, it looks like you're happily married, after all,' Betty said sarcastically.

He couldn't find any civil thing to say to her, so he just shook his head at her.

'What?' she said. 'Just saying it how it looks.'

'Leave us alone, Betty,' he said, moving away from her.

He broke into a run, catching up to Brigid as she struggled to get her suitcase in the car.

'Brigid, you shouldn't be lifting that so soon. You'll hurt yourself.'

'*Piss off*, Alex!' she sobbed, wedging the suitcase into the boot of the car. 'Like you give a damn about me. You're off kissing other women.' Alex felt the sting of Brigid's hand slapping against his cheek. 'How long did you remain faithful for, Alex? Six weeks? Or did you jump straight into it?'

He held onto her wrist, strong enough to stop her hitting him again, but not hard enough to hurt her. He could never hurt Brigid. 'That's not fair, Brigid. I've never cheated on you and I never will.'

'I saw you kissing her!'

'Did you see me push her off me, too? She kissed *me*, Brigid. I didn't want that.'

A fresh tear rolled down Brigid's cheek. Alex moved his hand to wipe it off, but she slapped his hand away. '*Excuses*! Is that … her? Your ex?'

Alex nodded slowly.

'She's p—pregnant.'

He nodded again. 'It's not mine.'

Brigid clenched her jaw. 'Why would she be here if it wasn't?'

He sighed. 'She thinks it's mine, but I know it's not. We're going to get a paternity test done to prove it.'

'What if it is?' Her question was a whisper. He might not have heard it if he hadn't been standing so close to her.

He cupped her face in his hands. 'It doesn't change anything between us.'

She shook her head slowly, pulling his hands from her face. 'It changes everything, Alex.' She dropped her gaze to the ground, refusing to look him in the eye. 'M—maybe you'd be better off with her.'

'Brigid—'

'She's *pregnant*, Alex. And it could be *your* child.' The tears were rolling freely down her face now, and he was certain his heart had stopped beating. 'I can't compete with that. I can't give you a … a family, Alex. I want to, but I can't. So, yes, m—maybe you'd be better off with h—her.'

Without glancing back at him, she got into her car and turned the key in the ignition. He watched as she pulled away from the kerb and headed out of sight. His wife. Leaving him. And he had no idea where she was going, or if they'd ever make it past this. He'd taken Betty outside to try to make her leave, knowing it would make Brigid worry if she'd thought something was wrong. And somehow … *somehow* … it all went wrong. He could feel his breath caught in his chest, his heart breaking, and his mind running in circles making it impossible to think.

Maybe she'd been right to think they weren't meant to be together. He'd only brought her pain and turned her life upside down. But he was also still very much convinced that everything working against them being together and being happy only meant they should fight harder. Because he knew, if they could get through this, they could have something beautiful.

Betty might be able to carry a child, but he could never be a family with her. He didn't love Betty. He loved Brigid. He was head-over-heels in love with the fiery red-head he'd just let drive away from him. They didn't need kids of their own to be a family. *She* was his family. *She* was all he needed. *She* had become the air he needed to breathe.

And now, he was losing her quicker than oxygen

being burned up in a wildfire.

Chapter 19

Brigid stared at the ceiling of her old room. She'd been sceptical about whether or not her daddy would let her come home. But when he saw her on the doorstep, her suitcase next to her and her eyes red from crying, he pulled her into his arms and held her. He'd respected her privacy, not asking questions until she was ready to talk. But she wasn't sure when that would be.

She'd made herself scarce over the last few days, staying in her room, emerging only to use the bathroom. At least once a day, Colleen had brought in a meal and made her eat it, but otherwise her appetite was gone. She missed Alex. She wanted to give him everything he wanted, but she couldn't. She'd never be able to. She wanted to love him for the rest of her life, making memories and doing life with him. But she would be holding him back.

He could have a family with someone else—if not with Betty. He could be happy. And she wanted him to be happy, even if it broke her heart. Sure, they'd gotten married so Alex could gain citizenship and keep the inn—her part of the arrangement no longer existed. But he would be getting his papers soon. Would that even matter? If he got back together with Betty, would they stay here, or would they go back to Paris? Maybe he wouldn't care about the inn—or her—if Betty was having his child. Would he always remember Brigid, or would she just be a stain in his past he'd rather forget?

Brigid groaned and rolled onto her side. The very thought of losing Alex sent a pain through her chest. Her heart was already broken. Losing him would ruin her. She couldn't even imagine feeling the same way she felt for Alex with anyone else. Maybe she was destined to be alone. It would break her, but she knew what she had to do. She just wished it didn't have to be the only way.

Colleen knocked lightly on her door and came in, a bowl of soup in her hands. 'Your rations are here,' she said. 'Come on, sit up.'

'I'm not hungry,' Brigid moaned, pulling a pillow over her face.

'I don't care.' Colleen pulled the pillow off Brigid and placed the bowl of soup on the bedside table. 'You've been moping in here for three days and you haven't told either of us why.'

'I'm not ready to,' she said, sitting up.

Colleen sat on the edge of Brigid's bed. 'You don't have to tell Daddy yet, he's all for giving space,' she said. 'But I'm not. So, talk.'

Brigid took a shaky breath, hugging a pillow to her stomach, her vision blurring with tears. 'I have to let him go.'

Colleen shook her head. 'Brigid—'

'I have to, Colleen, it's not fair on him. I can't—' She swiped at a tear. 'I can't give him a family, I'm a wreck, a—and now his ex is in town and she's pregnant.'

'Is it … his?'

Brigid shrugged her shoulders, sobbing. 'He doesn't think so, but they're getting a test done.'

'Okay, so you'll know for sure,' Colleen said, taking hold of Brigid's hand. 'But there's no point beating yourself up about it until you do.'

'You don't get it, Colleen. I can't give him kids. And I'm broken, I—'

'Does he even want kids?'

'Of course he does.'

'Have you asked him?'

Brigid blinked back a tear. Was it something she had to ask him? She guessed she'd just assumed he wanted kids since he proposed their arrangement in the first place. Then again, they had mentioned having kids of their own before … this. And he'd seemed excited about the idea. But how would he feel about it now?

'God, Brigid,' Colleen continued. 'Have you even

talked to him about it?'

'Yes, we've talked.' She sighed, squeezing the pillow. 'Before everything happened. But he wanted more kids and I ... can't. I just can't. I wish it was different, but I ...' *Can't.* She couldn't even finish the sentence again, it hurt so much. 'There's nothing I can do about it, Colleen. But it doesn't mean I have to stop him from moving on with someone else.'

Colleen sighed. 'You need to talk to him.' Brigid furrowed her brow, looking up at her sister. 'Hear me out—he said he wanted kids before you got stabbed, but he might not now. You can't just hide out in here, avoiding him forever. He's a good guy, Brigid, and you're probably tearing him apart by ignoring him.'

Brigid scoffed, though in her heart she wished it was true. 'I think you're exaggerating. He's probably already moved on.'

Colleen picked up Brigid's phone and turned the screen on, proving her wrong with all the missed calls from Alex.

'Doesn't look like he's moved on.'

Brigid sighed. 'Most of those calls were on Wednesday,' she stated, taking the phone back. 'And some yesterday. None of those were today.'

'If you hadn't recently been stabbed, I'd slap you,' Colleen said. 'That doesn't mean he's losing interest. It means he's giving you time. Brigid, I saw him while you were in surgery. He was worried sick, and he never left. You guys might have some crazy arrangement that may or may not still be applicable, but he cares about you. *A lot*.'

Brigid blinked back another tear. 'It didn't look like it when he was kissing his ex,' she whispered.

'Give him a chance.'

***

Alex stared at the envelope Betty had given him, totally unsure of how he felt. Did he want to know what the result was? What if it was positive? What if he was the father after all? He'd already told Betty he'd still like her to leave, but he'd also felt guilty for thinking he might be turning his back on his child. More than anything, he wished he wasn't in this situation. He wanted Brigid in every way possible, but he was starting to feel she didn't want him.

He'd tried calling her to beg her to listen to him make excuses, shift the blame. But the truth is, he could've stopped Betty from kissing him. But he didn't. And that scared him. Was there a small part of him that still cared for Betty, regardless of how much she'd screwed him over? Was there a part of him that had hoped she would show up on his doorstep and beg him to take her back? He'd never thought about it, but Brigid's absence was making him paranoid.

He'd called her less often the second day she was gone—he didn't want to keep annoying her if she didn't want to talk to him. But he didn't want to make excuses or even try to explain things he couldn't. He just wanted her to come home.

He hadn't called her today. He knew they were supposed to get the paternity test results back—maybe it was his subconscious refusing to call Brigid. What if the child was his? What if Brigid decided to hear him out before they got the results? If the child was his, it could just make things messy. So, he decided to take a different approach. He knew Brigid was staying at her daddy's place—he'd seen her car while he drove the streets trying to find her. Regardless of what the results were, he planned to call in and talk to her face to face, begging her to give him a chance. He may not be sure about Betty and the child, but he was certain he needed Brigid in his life. And they couldn't just be friends—it would kill him.

Holding his breath, he opened the envelope and unfolded the paper inside, scanning the page until his eyes fell to the single word that had the power to let him move on with Brigid or turn his life upside-down.

Negative.

The breath he was holding onto rushed out of him in relief. He was not the father. He was right all along, but more than that, he could get Brigid back. They didn't need to worry about this coming between them. They could move on. He felt his heart pounding in his chest. He had to see Brigid now—he couldn't wait until later. He couldn't give her the whole day like he'd planned to. He wanted to take her in his arms and kiss her senseless and make love to her until the morning sun shone through their window. But he couldn't push her. They had to talk first. They had to start again.

'Alex?'

Alex flicked his eyes up to meet Betty's. Did he look as relieved as he felt? 'It's negative.'

Betty sighed. 'I know. I looked.'

'Did you know?'

She dropped her gaze. 'I'd figured it was his, but I'd hoped it was yours.'

'He left you when he found out, didn't he?'

She nodded, a tear rolling down her cheek and dropping off her chin, landing in a soft splatter on the floorboards. 'I thought if it was yours, you'd forgive me—for the sake of the child.'

Alex shook his head. 'Then you don't know me at all, Betty,' he said. 'I would have wanted to be a part of the child's life, but not as your partner. And I'd never leave Brigid for you.'

'Not even if she left you?' Betty's eyes looked hopeful, but deep down, he knew she already knew the answer.

'She won't leave me. I'll make sure of it.'

Betty sighed, swiped at a tear, and smiled. 'You really have something special with her, don't you?'

Alex nodded. 'I almost lost her, Betty, and it almost killed me. I knew it then, and I know it now. What we have might be … complicated, of sorts, but I love her. And that's never going to change.'

Betty swallowed. 'I'm happy for you, Alex, I am. And I'm sorry I caused more stress for you both. I really had no idea you were married now.' She sighed. 'God, I must look like a fool—travelling all the way here to try to win you back over a child that's not yours. I'm—I'll just get the next flight out. I'm sorry, again, Alex. I really didn't mean any harm.'

Alex smiled. He knew they could never really be friends. But at least they were leaving on good terms. 'Good luck with the kid,' he said. 'And the other guy, if he mans up.'

Brigid nodded, smiling back. 'You too, with Brigid. Don't stop fighting for her.'

'I don't plan on it.'

***

'Brigid, Alex is at the door and you have to answer it.'

Brigid blinked at Colleen. 'Can't you deal with him?'

Colleen grabbed hold of Brigid's arm and pulled her towards the door. 'He's *your* husband, and if he's anything like I know he is, he's not going to leave until he talks to you. So, no, I won't deal with him. *You* will.'

Brigid groaned as Colleen dragged her to the front door and let her sister straighten her clothes, tucking stray hairs in, presumably to make her look more presentable.

Colleen sighed. 'He's seen you at your worst, anyway, but still—it doesn't hurt to try.' She reached out and gave Brigid's cheeks a hard pinch as there was another knock at the door.

Brigid brought her hands to her cheeks. 'Ow!

What was that for?'

Colleen shrugged. 'I've seen it on movies. It's supposed to give your cheeks a natural blush.'

'What if I don't want a natural blush?'

'Well … too bad.' Colleen grimaced. 'Maybe I pinched a bit hard.'

'Go on,' Brigid said, shooing her sister. 'Go find something else to terrorise.'

She waited until Colleen ducked out of sight, knowing she was probably still within earshot, and rubbed her cheeks to try to ease the lingering pain. She took a shaky breath and opened the door slowly, feeling the breath knocked out of her once she saw him.

God, her fantasies didn't do him justice. He looked like he'd been working on the inn—he was wearing his flannelette shirt and his jeans that made him look sexier than they were probably supposed to. His hair was tousled and looked as though he'd ran his fingers through it in an attempt to look neater. Had he been on his way over and thought he should have neatened up a little? She figured it didn't matter how he was dressed, he still looked—and smelled—amazing. It only made it harder for her to go through with her plan.

'Hey, Brigid,' he said, an uncertain smile tugging at his lips.

Even the way he said her name made her heart swoon, the tone of his voice reverberating through her body, warming every inch of her. She urged herself to say something—anything. She had to keep it together. *Hi*—that would be a good start. Her lips parted, but nothing came out. Alex rubbed his hands together.

'Can I come inside?'

'Umm …' Brigid looked back inside, certain she'd caught a glimpse of Colleen ducking back behind the wall. She stepped outside, closing the door behind her. 'Colleen's inside,' she said. 'I'm pretty sure she's trying to eavesdrop.'

'All right.' He took a shaky breath. 'I—' His expression changed to puzzled as he studied her face. 'Are you all right?'

'Hmm?'

He shook his head slowly, reaching his hand out and brushing his thumb over her cheek. His touch sent sparks shooting into her chest, her resolve dissipating every second his thumb lingered against her. 'Your cheeks are red.'

She could feel the blush forming on her already reddened cheeks. She covered her cheeks with her hands and glanced away. His hand dropped to his side.

'Oh, Colleen's fault,' she said, her voice shaky. 'I— I'm … umm … your calls … s—sorry.'

God, that had sounded much clearer in her head. Why was her brain having difficulty in relaying the message to her mouth? If he'd just stop looking at her like that—a smile tugging at his lips, his eyes round and flashing, his eyebrows pulled together in a look somewhere between amused and concerned.

'What?'

His smile widened, bearing his teeth. 'Nothing,' he said. 'I just ... I missed you, Brigid.'

'Oh.'

Oh? Surely, there was something else she could say. But, what? Anything she'd planned to say over the last few days had been wiped from her memory the second she laid eyes on him. And without the reasoning that she'd had, suggesting they divorce was sounding completely ridiculous.

He let out a deep breath, the smile wiped from his face. He dropped his gaze to his hands. 'I ... umm ... the baby—' He flicked his eyes up to meet hers. 'It's not mine.'

She blinked, a wave of relief washing over her, followed by a clenching on her heart. The baby wasn't his. Had he come just to tell her that? Or maybe the very thought that he could have had a child made him think about a future with Brigid—and what it wouldn't hold.

'Are ... are you happy?'

He nodded slowly. 'Relieved. I didn't want it to come between us.' He took her hands in his.

'And Betty?' she said.

'On her way home,' he said, the smile returning. 'I set her straight.' He lifted one of her hands, pressing his lips against the back of her fingers.

It broke her heart. Just because Betty was gone, and the child wasn't his didn't take away the fact that they wouldn't be able to have children together. She had nothing to offer him in return for everything he offered her with their marriage.

'Alex,' she whispered.

He squeezed her hands and held her gaze. 'I tried to think of excuses, Brigid,' he said. 'I couldn't explain why she showed up, or what she wanted, because I didn't really know. But I ran through all kinds of scenarios in my head of what I could say to reassure you and I—' He paused for a breath and swallowed. 'I couldn't do that to you, Brigid. I couldn't make up excuses because you deserve better than that.'

He thought she deserved better? Right now, she didn't feel like she deserved anything. She opened her mouth, trying to force something out, but no words came. She couldn't even process anything she could potentially say—anything to make it better or to … end it. But Colleen's words still rang through her head. Alex cared about her. He didn't want to give her excuses. He gave her time. And here he was, on her doorstep, talking it out. She couldn't just jump to conclusions. But then again, he was doing all this for her—and for what? She couldn't give him kids. Their future was bleak. Heck, she'd been nothing but evasive and a terrible patient to him since she'd been stabbed. *He* deserved better.

'And then I thought this didn't need excuses,' he continued, oblivious of the fact that her breaths were quick and shallow. 'Because nothing happened. She was out for something and she didn't get it. She didn't mean to come between us. She was surprised to even find out I was married.'

'Alex,' she said, her voice shaking.

'But she's gone, Brigid. There is nothing with her.

I just got the results, and I came straight here. I figured I had to tell you face to face, I had to … see you … because it's been driving me cr—'

'Alex, I want a divorce.'

***

Alex stopped talking, letting the words catch up to him, praying she hadn't said what he thought she said. Her lips were parted, her breath shallow, her eyes glistening. Had he missed something? Had he read the signs all wrong? Had he just got a bit too excited about her opening the door to him and letting him talk that he'd misread everything?

'*What*?'

She dropped her eyes, a tear rolling down her cheek. 'I think it's for the best,' she whispered.

So, he hadn't misheard her. *Divorce*. He released her hands, folding one arm across his chest and holding his chin in his other hand. He squeezed his eyes closed and pinched the bridge of his nose. Was he supposed to do something differently? Was he not supposed to give her time? Was he supposed to pester her with excuses? When he opened his eyes, her arms were crossed, and she was staring at the ground.

'It's not going to work, Alex,' she said. 'We can't … work.'

'We haven't even been able to give this a chance, Brigid.'

'I know, it's just … I—'

'No.'

'It shouldn't be a lengthy process,' she continued. 'It's not like we've … consummated … the marriage.'

'*No*,' he repeated. She looked up at him and he could see it was tearing her apart as much as it was breaking his heart. 'It's not happening.'

'Alex—'

'Damn it, Brigid! I nearly lost you.' He stepped closer cupping her face in his hands, brushing one of her tears aside. His vision was blurring from tears of his own threatening. 'The thought that I could have lost you it … it almost killed me, Brigid. I didn't … I couldn't …'

She sobbed, leaning against his chest. He wrapped his arms around her, holding her close. This wasn't going to be the last time he held her. It couldn't be. He couldn't let her go.

'I'm sorry,' she whispered into his chest between sobs. 'I have to … I—I'm sorry.'

She pulled away, and he reluctantly let her, his mind spinning, swirling with ideas to keep her. He could kidnap her, make her spend time with him so he could convince her to stay. He could keep banging on her door until she gave him another chance. He could buy out every florist in town and fill her room with flowers. He could take her in his arms and kiss her until she changed her mind. God, anything. But he couldn't move. He couldn't force her to change her mind because he couldn't live without her. She was about to close the door between them when he stuck his foot between the door and the doorframe.

She glanced up at him.

'Tomorrow night,' he said. 'Come to the inn. I'll make dinner for us and we can talk about it. If you still want a divorce by the end of it, we'll do it.'

'Alex,' she whispered.

'I'm not going to let you go this easy, Brigid,' he said. 'Have dinner with me.'

He waited for what felt like an eternity for her response. But when it barely came out of her mouth, and he let the door close between them, he'd felt like it was this or nothing.

'All right.'

Chapter 20

She was giving him a chance.

Well, she'd agreed to give him a chance. And he only had this one to convince her to stay with him. God, he'd never thought he'd be begging his wife to stay with him after being married for less than two months. In fact, he'd hoped he'd never have to beg his wife to stay with him. He'd always planned on treating her right, spoiling her, making her feel loved and special. He never wanted to give her a reason to leave him.

But here he was. Waiting for her to come to dinner so he could give her all the reasons why she should stay.

How was he even supposed to do that after such a short time? At least after twenty years, you have history. You have legitimate reasons. His only reason was to give them a go since they haven't had the chance to yet. But he couldn't stop thinking about Brigid's reasons. Why did she want a divorce? Was it something he did? Something he said? Something he should have said or done?

He lit the candles on the table he'd set. It was a cool night, so he'd pulled a table over near the fireplace and set it up there. At least if they had enough of sitting at the table, they could sit on the couches and still be warm. Ailbe had left for the night and no one else was at the inn. They had the place to themselves. Alex took a shaky breath, scanning the room. The last time they'd had the place mostly to themselves, Brigid ended up getting stabbed.

At least that wouldn't happen this time.

He couldn't say the same for himself, since Brigid would be wielding a sharp steak knife over dinner and Alex had no idea why she wanted a divorce. Or what lengths she'd go to to get one.

He checked the time—she should be here any minute. He had the steaks keeping warm in the oven, the salad on the table, a nice merlot breathing between the plates. He didn't have a huge repertoire of meals he could cook well, but he did feel he made quite the mean steak. It was all in the seasoning and the turning, he felt. Season the steak, cook it slowly, turn once. But he knew his fabulous steak wouldn't be enough to change Brigid's mind. He just had to hear her out. And then, commence begging.

Had he ever begged for anything in his life? He'd

always worked hard for anything he wanted. And Brigid was no exception. Except he might actually drop down to his knees and beg her if he had to.

'Get a grip,' he mumbled.

If Brigid wanted to leave, he shouldn't beg her to stay. More than anything, he wanted her to be happy. He'd just prefer if she was happy with him. There was a saying he'd heard—if you love someone, let them go. He scoffed. It had to be the biggest load of bull he'd ever heard. He'd always known when to fight for something. And Brigid was worth fighting for. But there had to be a line somewhere and, as much as he hated to admit it, maybe they were at that line. God, he hoped not. He might have actually preferred if Darcy had killed him instead of living a life without Brigid.

The door nudged open and he took a shaky breath. She was here. And she looked a vision, like she'd stepped straight out of one of his fantasy dreams. She shrugged off her jacket, granting him a view of her slender shoulders, adorned only by the spaghetti straps of her elegant violet knee-length dress and her soft curls that fell over them. Her cheeks tinged with a blush he only assumed was from the cool breeze outside. She moved towards him, her hips swaying with each step, stirring something inside him—something deep, something primal. God, he'd just about beg right now. There was no way he was letting this woman slip through his fingers.

'Hi,' she said, her voice breathy, nervous. She was

sexy as hell.

'You look beautiful.'

He pressed his lips against her cheek and heard her take a shaky breath as he took her coat, draping it over the back of a nearby couch. He rolled his sleeves up, feeling the room heat up already. Was the fire too hot? It hadn't been, until Brigid came into the room. He pulled the chair out for her and waited for her to sit. He poured a glass of wine and handed it to her.

'I'll be right back,' he said.

He didn't wait for a reply before he moved to the kitchen to get the steaks, ignoring the urge to step outside to let the cool air calm his body down. She wasn't dressed like someone who wanted a divorce. Which would make him feel even worse if she decided she still wanted one.

He wanted—*needed*—Brigid.

And letting her go would be the end of him.

***

Small talk.

That's all she could manage. It's all *they* could manage. And she knew why.

It's because they knew how this was going to end.

Before they'd been involved, she'd had no trouble expressing her opinion. Neither of them had a problem with saying what they thought. They could talk about things, do things without arguing.

Relatively. Then she got stabbed and everything changed. It had seemed like Alex was walking on eggshells around her, and she didn't blame him. She wasn't exactly doing or saying anything to make it easier for him. She'd hoped they might have been able to start talking normally again, and maybe they could have. If she hadn't said she wanted a divorce.

God, she hadn't even meant to say it when she did. All of Colleen's convincing to give him a chance and him showing up on her doorstep trying to explain the unexplainable, she'd almost been convinced out of it. But then she had to open her mouth and have the wrong thing come out.

There's no wonder they mostly ate in silence, talking only about the cold outside and how nice his steak was. Honestly, it was the best damn steak she'd ever had, but she still felt like she couldn't enjoy it fully. Not when there was this tension between them. Not when there was the one topic they'd agreed to talk about that they were both avoiding.

Alex topped her glass up and dished another healthy serving of salad on his plate. She studied the bit of salad still on her own plate, noticing all the different ingredients, the colours, a combination of strong individual flavours amalgamated together to form a unique flavour of its own.

She gasped. This wasn't his first salad. She glanced up at him, his eyebrows raised, a questioning look on his face.

'What's wrong?' he said, taking another

mouthful.

'I thought you don't like salad,' she said, squinting.

He stopped chewing, dropping his gaze to the salad bowl between them.

'When you came over for dinner,' she continued, prompting him. 'I said I made the salad and you said you didn't like salad.'

He nodded slowly, swallowing the mouthful he had. 'I did say that, didn't I?'

'Yes, you did,' she said. 'And now you've made this amazing salad, and something tells me it's not the first time you've done it.'

He placed the cutlery onto the plate and folded his arms on the table, leaning closer to her. He cleared his throat. 'Well, since you're my *wife*, I guess you're entitled to know my secret.'

Secret? She raised an eyebrow. He let out a shaky sigh she was sure was more put on than realistic.

'I like salad.'

She waited a moment, squinting at him, waiting for more. He spread his hands out between them, picked up his fork, and shovelled another mouthful of salad into his mouth.

'*That's* your secret?'

He nodded.

'You like salad. How is that a secret?'

'Honestly, I prefer it over vegetables as a side,' he said. 'It just didn't sound very manly, saying I like salads.'

She laughed. 'What if I'd spent the rest of our

lives making vegetables for you instead of salad?'

A smile tugged at his lips, making her heart flip. 'Then I still would have eaten it and said it was the most delicious meal I've ever had.'

'Even if it was bad?'

He nodded.

'What if I'd managed to burn it all to a crisp?'

'It'd still be amazing.'

'How so?'

The mischievous flashing in his eyes calmed, his eyes growing serious, deep, warming her inside while, at the same time, sending a shiver down her spine. 'Because it would mean you're still with me.'

Her mouth fell open and she bowed her head, squeezing her eyes shut. Did he really mean that? She heard the gentle clatter of his fork being placed on his plate again and the sliding of his chair. His footsteps, moving around the table and stopping next to her. She felt his touch as he gently took the knife and fork from her hands and turned her to face him. She fluttered her eyes open, the intense look on his face catching her breath. He was squatting down, one knee resting on the ground, both of her hands in his.

'Alex,' she whispered, blinking back a tear.

'Brigid, I—' He lifted one hand and brushed a tear from her face. 'I couldn't stop thinking about it. You. Us. I can't work out where it all went wrong—the moment where we lost it.'

'Did we ever really have it?' she whispered, another tear rolling down her cheek. God, she wished this could be easier.

He swallowed, nodding his head, his lips pressed together. 'I felt it—I *feel* it. Don't you?'

He brushed the tear away with his thumb, caressing the length of her chin with his touch. The touch that started a fire blazing through her body, her yearning for him more pressing than ever before. She nodded, staring into his eyes. She could see him—all of him. It's as though he'd opened up to her in a way he hadn't before. She could see the sincerity in his eyes. The hope. The passion. The love. She couldn't let that go. She couldn't let *him* go. Even though she'd fought it all along, he'd become the air she needed to breath, the ground beneath her feet, her support, her strength. Her everything. Colleen was right—he'd seen her at her worst, and he was still here, kneeling in front of her.

His eyes glistened, his eyebrows pinched together. 'God, Brigid,' he said, his voice breaking. 'I was going to beg you if it came to it, but I … I don't have to, do I?'

She shook her head, swallowing the tears that were choking her. 'I can't give you kids, Alex,' she whispered. 'It's not fair on you. You could have a family with someone else. Y—you could be happy.' She swiped at her tears with the back of her hand.

He dropped to both of his knees and slid closer to her, his chest against her bare legs. She could feel the warmth of his body underneath his clothes and she wanted nothing more than to feel him—all of him. His body moving against hers. Nothing between them but the passion they shared. He cupped her face between his warm hands, gentle, but so masculine. God, he was making it impossible to resist him.

'I couldn't be happier with anyone else, Brigid.'

'Why not?' she sobbed.

He nudged her chin, his eyes begging her to look at him, to understand him. Believe him. 'They're not you,' he said. 'I know we talked about having kids of our own, but if it's not in the cards, it doesn't mean I don't want to be with you.' He dropped his hands to her hips and nudged her towards him, her knees sliding to the side to let him closer. 'We don't need kids to be a family—you're my family. You're all I need. I love *you*, Brigid, not anyone else.'

She felt her mouth drop open at his words, her heart skipping a beat and her breath catching in her throat. He … loves … her? Had he meant to say it, or had it slipped out in the moment? His eyes were still sincere, his expression unchanged from the one she was fighting not to give in to.

'What did you say?' she whispered.

'I mean, if we want to extend the family *that* way, there are other options,' he said.

'Not that bit.'

A smile tugged at his lips—the adorable smile that had made her fall for him and made it impossible to really leave him. 'I love you,' he said, matter-of-factly. 'I almost lost you, Brigid, in the hospital. I can't lose you again. It would actually kill me. You drive me crazy, but I don't want to be away from you for even a second longer. You're the most incredible woman I've ever met, and I gave you my heart the second I laid eyes on you, even if you didn't realise it.'

'Alex, I—' She tried to finish the sentence, but she was still trying to convince herself this was actually happening.

'Just tell me you won't leave me,' he said, his voice pleading. 'Please, Brigid.'

'I love you,' she whispered. His eyes widened, and she could see his pulse on the soft spot of his neck. She wanted to see how it felt pulsing against her lips. She moved her hands to the back of his neck, letting her thumb slide over that spot she found so alluring. 'God, I love you.'

Before she could say anything more, his lips were on hers and his hands were sliding her off the chair and onto his lap. She parted her legs, positioning them either side of his body to be closer to him. His tongue parted her lips and she let him in, her tongue dancing with his with as much passion and attention as he gave her. She heard the growl at the base of his throat as she slid closer to him, pressing her body against his chest, and felt desire and wanting shoot through her and to her core as he cupped her ass, pressing her harder against him.

There was no mistaking it.

She needed him.

And she needed him now.

***

He felt her shiver as he tugged her dress above her hips and slid his thumbs beneath the top of her panties. He felt his jeans tighten as she dropped her head back and moaned as he left a trail of nips and kisses down her neck and to the mounds of her breasts. God, she smelled amazing. A mixture of her unique smell, her tempting perfume, and her desire. He needed more. He slid his hands up her body, squeezing her hips as they moved, bringing her dress up and over her head.

Her hands slid down his chest, working at the buttons quicker than it took him to get them done up. He ran his hands over her lace bra, following it to the clip at the back and flicked it apart as she got the last of the buttons undone. He shrugged out of his shirt as she flung her bra to the floor, her breasts hiding modestly behind her soft curls. She was the most perfect thing he'd ever laid eyes on. She flung her arms around his neck, her lips pressing against his, her tongue telling his a secret that dripped with temptation, invitation, and everything dirty.

It made him wild.

Wild for her. Wild for her taste, her touch. Wild with the primal need to claim every part of her as his, to love her until they passed out from exhaustion, only to start again when they awoke. She was it for him. If they just didn't have the last layers of clothing between them …

He felt her shift her weight, urging him to lay down on the ground and, as if reading his mind, she slid her hands down his body, her lips following behind them until her fingers met with the button of his jeans. She'd made even quicker work of that than any of the buttons on his shirt—not that he was complaining—and tugged his pants down until she'd had them and his shoes off. He heard her take a shaky breath and he propped himself up on his elbows, admiring the beautiful specimen that was resting on her knees beside him, even if her arms were folded lazily across her chest.

'Everything all right?' he asked, trying to ignore the obvious throbbing occurring in the lower part of him.

'I just—I …' She let out another shaky breath, a hint of a laugh lacing through it. 'I dreamed of this. Of what it would be like. With you. I … I didn't think I'd ever know. I mean, we were rudely interrupted last time we … tried.'

He pulled himself into a seated position and cupped her cheek with one of his hands. 'We're the only ones here tonight, Brigid.' He pressed a kiss to her lips, allowing himself to linger and taste her delicateness. 'The place is ours.'

The timidness that was in her eyes was replaced with the wild look that stole his heart when he first met her. The nervous, modest Brigid who had knelt next to him was taken over by the wild Brigid—the one who knew what she wanted and how to take it. And he would let her take it, all of it. But not before he gave her the attention she craved—needed.

He rose to his feet, pulling Brigid up with him.

'Since we don't have proper heating installed upstairs yet, I think down here would be best.'

She glanced behind him. 'The couch looks too small,' she said.

He felt his smile widen as he leaned close to her ear. 'Who said anything about the couch?'

He pulled away, catching a glimpse of her widened eyes as he set to work, laying a blanket on the floor in front of the fireplace and placing the throw pillows on top of it.

He stretched one hand out towards her, presenting his setup with the other.

'Milady.'

She took his hand and walked over to the middle of his make-shift bed and sat down. 'You certainly have a way with words, Mr Carter,' she said, flicking her eyes up at him in a way that sent a fresh wave of desire washing over him.

He joined her on the blanket. 'As do you, Mrs Carter.'

On all fours, he pressed his lips to hers again, searching her mouth, tasting, teasing, until he was certain he'd never forget her taste. He lifted one hand and cradled her neck as she leaned back against the pillows, stretching her legs beneath him. He rested his body against hers, careful not to put too much weight on her. She was, after all, still recovering. And, until she was ready for more, this would have to be slow.

He kissed her neck, brushing her soft hair to the side with his fingertips as his hands explored her body, feeling her warmth and desire radiating from her skin. Her perfect, delicious skin that he never wanted to take his hands off. He felt her legs clench around his thigh and the gentle movements of her body as he kissed across her collarbone and every perfect inch of her breasts, sucking the peaks into his mouth, and teasing her with his tongue as he moved. Once he was sure both of her breasts had been given enough attention, he kissed down her belly, licking, tasting, until he reached her scar.

He traced the line with his fingertips and pressed his lips against every little part of it. God, he hoped it didn't still cause her pain. He wished he could make it all disappear with his kisses. But even so, it only made her more beautiful because it represented the strength she had to be able to go through what she did. She was strong, but he would protect her for the rest of his life. And he would never stop loving this incredible woman.

He hovered his lips over her skin, sliding down the few agonising inches to meet the thin material of her panties. He tucked his fingers underneath the elastic and tugged them down, moving his body and leaving kisses down her legs until the panties were off. He slid his hands back up her legs until he met her warmth, his kisses following, tasting all of her. Every squirm and every moan she did had him closer to losing himself in all that was her, but he held back, knowing she was close. He could feel her body tightening around his fingers and felt her hand tighten around his wrist when it was becoming too much.

'Alex, please.' She pulled at his arm, pulling him up towards her, kissing him impatiently.

He didn't need to be asked twice.

He slid his briefs off and hovered his body over hers, looking into her eyes, fighting with himself to not lose control. Her eyes darkened with the same desire he felt, and the tone of her voice was all he needed to lose himself.

'I need you,' she said.

He kissed her passionately, sliding into her warmth, moving his body against hers, her moans and movements pushing him dangerously close to the edge. He felt her body tighten and pulse and heard his name whispered on her lips as she glided down from her high, his own body flying with hers.

He was home.

And she was his everything.

Chapter 21

Ten months later …

'Alex! Where the *hell* is that dog?'

Alex glanced towards Brigid, nudging the little brown terrier into his office. She was fuming, storming down the stairs with one shoe on and the other in her hand. *Shoot*. He smiled a defensive smile as she came to a stop in front of him.

'Where is he?' she said.

He shook his head. 'How do you even know it was him?'

She waved the shoe between them. 'I don't see any other dog getting around the inn eating shoes, do you?'

'Mmm, but how do you know it was a dog?' He

slid his hands around her waist tugging her closer.

'Have you suddenly taken on a shoe-eating fetish?'

He waggled his eyebrows, but she remained unimpressed. 'I could have.'

'This was my last pair of nice shoes, Alex. He even chewed up my slippers last week.'

He pressed a kiss against her cheek, across to her chin and down her neck as she dropped her head back. 'I'll buy you some more,' he whispered, kissing the soft spot under her ear. 'But for now, if you look in the bottom drawer of the front desk, you'll find your emergency pair of shoes.'

She moaned as he pulled away. 'If he hasn't found them, too.'

'Hey, you know you can't stay mad at him,' he teased. 'I think you love him more than you love me.'

'Is that so?' she raised an eyebrow, pushing onto her tip-toes to nibble his earlobe. 'Do I need to give you more attention, so you don't feel like I'm favouring the small, defenceless puppy hiding in your office?'

He could feel his jeans tightening as he held her close. 'Oh, I need lots of attention.'

He heard her delicious chuckle that made him want to take her here and now, despite there being people around them. 'Tonight, my darling,' she said, tapping her fingers on his chest before turning away and walking towards the front desk, her hips swaying.

He exhaled, trying to regain control of the part of

his body that went rogue, and pushed into his office. He looked at the dog, sitting in the corner, chewing on Alex's emergency pair of shoes, and shook his head.

'You're costing me a fortune, you know that?' He scratched the dog on his head and settled down in front of his computer to answer Scott's video call.

'Alex Carter,' Scott said. 'I thought I'd never hear from you again.'

'It's been busy,' Alex said. He'd been missing all of Scott's calls lately and, when he tried to return them, he never got an answer. It was like a big game of phone-tennis.

'Brigid hasn't divorced you yet?' Scott teased.

He shook his head. 'Thankfully not. What about Olivia?'

'She puts up with me,' Scott said, a smile tugging at his lips. 'Actually, we've got some news.'

'Oh, yeah? We've got news, too.' Alex tapped his leg and the mischievous terrier dropped the shoe and raced over to him.

Scott leaned closer to the camera and held up a small black and white photograph. It was difficult to make out, but there was no mistaking what that was. 'Meet mini me!'

'No way,' Alex said, letting out a laugh.

Scott nodded. 'Yep. Liv's about fifteen weeks. Do you think it looks like me?'

'I think you'd rather it looked like Olivia,' Alex teased.

Scott laughed and flipped him the bird. 'Anyway,

what's your news.'

'We have a recent addition to our family.'

Scott's eyes widened. 'Really? Olivia will be so—'

He lifted the dog onto his lap in view of the camera. 'Meet Scooter.'

'*Scooter*?'

Alex nodded.

'Did you name a dog after me?'

Alex shrugged. 'Well, he reminded me a lot of you.'

'How so?'

'Well, he eats shoes and he's an asshole.'

'I don't eat shoes!'

'Aha! So, you admit you're an asshole!'

Scott laughed, leaning towards the camera again. 'Only to you, my friend,' he said. 'Say hi to Brigid for us.'

'Will do. And congratulations about the baby.'

He ended the call, placed Scooter back on the floor and studied the paperwork on his desk. Bills. Wages. And enough incoming money to cover them all. He sighed and leaned back in his chair. It had been a big job renovating the inn. The whole place had been modernised while keeping the charm Brigid loved. They even extended it out to add an extra larger room upstairs—for Brigid and Alex—and two more offices downstairs. He smiled at the memory of the look on Ailbe's face as Alex told him that one of those offices was for him. He'd moved out of his broom cupboard and into his new office quicker than Alex could work out what to do next.

By the time the inn was finished, and he was adding the finishing touches, Brigid had had them fully booked for months in advance. The inn was becoming successful—it *was* successful—and he couldn't have done it without her. He was surrounded by the people he loved. He had Brigid. And their mischievous shoe-eating pooch. And they were waiting to hear from the adoption agency, though it could be a while.

It had been a year since he promised his life to Brigid. A year since his life changed forever—always for the better. Alex opened the drawer of his desk and pulled out a small box and moved towards the door of his office when the phone rang. He hesitated, considering letting it go through to the messages. But it was his direct line, not the bookings line. Reluctantly, he sighed, moving back towards his desk to answer the phone.

How was he to know it would change his life again?

***

'I hope you enjoy your stay at The Irish Maiden,' Brigid said, handing the room key to the couple who had just checked in and ignoring the phone ringing next to her. 'Just let me know if you need anything.'

She indicated for her assistant to take their bags upstairs for them, smiling at the thought. She had an *assistant*. Someone she could order around. Though, Alex referred to him as someone to help share the load so Brigid had more time on her hands. She sighed. Being married to the owner of the inn had its benefits after all—in so many ways. She smiled at the thought of giving Alex attention tonight like she'd promised, biting into her bottom lip. It *was* their anniversary, after all, and she may or may not have something special planned in the shape of a skimpy, rather revealing lace chemise. And her high-heeled shoes she kept out of reach of Scooter. As adorable as he was, they really had to work out a way to deal with his shoe fetish.

She registered Ailbe standing next to her, smelling fresh, and looking crisp in the new suit Alex had bought him. Even though her relationship had been somewhat restored with her own daddy, Ailbe was still very much like a father to her, and now, to Alex. The two of them always stirred each other up in ways only a father and son would. There'd even been people comment on their relationship. Of course, neither Alex or Ailbe denied being called father and son, and it only made her happier that her husband could have such a relationship with someone so special to her. *Husband*. She still felt like she was getting used to it—the very thought of it still made her blush.

Ailbe cleared his throat, drawing Brigid out of her thoughts. 'Ye gonna get that, lass?'

She squinted at him, briefly wondering what he was talking about before her ears picked up the ringing of the phone again.

'Oh! Right,' she said, placing her hand on the

phone. 'Thanks, Ailbe.'

He winked at her and grabbed a handful of the spare pens Alex insisted they keep at the front desk and went back to his office. She picked up the phone.

'The Irish Maiden, this is Brigid. How can I help you?'

'There's a package coming for you.'

She took a deep breath, knowing the voice all too well. She'd grown accustomed to the sexy smooth tone he talked with and, whether he spoke in person or over the phone, it still sent a warmth to her core. Even after a year.

'Look to your left,' he continued.

She obeyed, looking just in time to see Alex nudge Scooter out of his office and stand in the doorway. The little dog beelined towards her, a small package tied to his collar.

'That doesn't look big enough to be a new pair of shoes,' she teased.

Scooter came up to her feet and sat looking up at her, his tail wagging against the floor. She bent down and untied the box from his collar and gave him a pat. She opened the box to see a silver pendant— one of those naming ones. It had a large ring with two smaller rings within it, a small emerald hanging in the centre of them all. The larger ring had the names *Alex* and *Brigid* engraved on it. *Scooter* was engraved on the smallest ring, and the middle-sized one was blank. It was simple, yet so elegant. She loved it.

'Can you really stay mad at him?'

She kept the phone pressed to her ear, looked up at Alex and shook her head, a smile tugging at her lips. 'I suppose I can forgive him.'

She could see his smile from across the room. 'Do you like it?'

'I love it.'

'Happy anniversary, Mrs Carter.'

She blinked back the tears that were threatening to spill over the sweet gesture. 'Happy anniversary, Mr Carter.'

'I've got something to tell you,' Alex continued.

She furrowed her brow. He looked so serious. 'What is it?'

He pulled the phone away from his ear and hung up, indicating with a nod of his head for her to follow him outside. She placed the phone back on the holder and followed, Scooter trailing behind her. By the time she was outside, he was standing next to the corner of the porch that had collapsed before the renovations. She slid next to him and took in the masculine scent of all that was him as he draped his arm around her and pulled her close.

'Scott and Olivia are pregnant.'

He said it so matter-of-factly, but it still took Brigid by surprise. And also stirred a wave of jealousy through her. She'd never thought she could be excited for someone and also hurting with jealousy at the same time. She'd grown used to it—mostly. Seeing kids running around, pregnant women, or hearing baby talk. She'd learned to put on a brave face and accept it as fact. But she doubted time would ever heal the ache she felt. She cleared her throat and tried to put aside her feelings. This was exciting. Alex's best friend and his wife were pregnant. Brigid had the pleasure of meeting them when they came to stay at their grand reopening. They would make good parents.

'Wow.' She'd tried to say something reasonable, exciting, anything more than one word that sounded more like she was releasing a deep breath that had caught in her throat. But *wow* was all she could manage.

'But that's not all,' he continued, turning to face her, pulling her in for a deeper hug.

'Mmm?' She closed her eyes, her ear pressed to his chest, the smooth comforting rhythm of his heartbeat lulling her into a state of loving bliss.

'The adoption agency called.'

Her eyes shot open and she lingered a moment before looking up at him. The adoption agency? She'd expected it could be years before they heard from them again. Had their application been rejected after all their efforts to jump through the hoops?

'What did they say?' she said, feeling impatient that she even had to ask him to continue.

'Oh, not much.' He drew out the syllables and looked over the garden. 'They just wanted to discuss some information about a child.'

Child? She pulled away and whacked him on his arm. 'What are you saying, Alex?'

He glanced back at her, the mischievous smile on his face making her heart leap for more reasons than one. 'Specifically, a five-month old baby girl.'

Her mouth dropped open, and she was certain her heart stopped beating. He squinted, and tilted his head, his smile widening even more.

'Her name's Betha.'

'A—are you saying …?'

He nodded, cupping her face in his hands. 'She's ours, Brigid. We have a baby.'

A baby. Brigid felt her breaths quickening and the tears running down her face, her smile uncontrollable. Alex swept her up into his arms, holding her close, and pressed his lips against hers in a kiss that could bring anyone back to life. She could feel her every nerve on edge, vibrating with the excitement, yet still in unbelief. They were having a family. She was having a family—with Alex. And even if that little girl didn't come from Brigid's own body, she was certain Betha was going to be the most loved and cherished baby in town. She was theirs. Alex placed Brigid back on the ground and the world started spinning around her while looking clearer than it had ever been at the same time.

'Wh—when do we pick her up?' God, there was so much to get ready for.

'We can go right now, if you want,' Alex said, bringing her hands to his lips, and kissing every finger.

His eyes were dancing. The fact that he was just as excited as she was made her heart grow even more to accommodate the love she was feeling for him. And Betha. Their daughter.

'But we're not ready,' Brigid said, a list forming in her mind of what they needed to be ready for a baby. 'There's so much to buy and—'

Alex kissed her again, silencing her words and banishing her train of thought. When he broke the kiss, she was feeling dazed. He rested his forehead against hers. 'We'll figure it out. The adoption agency has the basics to last us a couple days. We can buy the necessities on our way to pick her up. And I might need your necklace back.'

'Hmm?'

'I know what name to put on the middle ring, now.'

She nodded, processing his words, and looked up at him. 'A baby,' she whispered.

He smiled, kissing her forehead. 'A baby.'

Brigid sighed. 'What do you think she looks like?'

Alex tilted his head to the side, his eyes still searching Brigid's face. He tucked a lock of hair behind her ear and brushed his fingertips across her cheek.

'I bet she has your eyes.'

Books by R. J. Groves

Thank you for reading!
I hope you enjoyed this
story as much as I did
writing it.
R. J. xx